Rappaccini's Daughter

Rappaccini's Daughter

Nathaniel Hawthorne

ET REMOTISSIMA PROPE

100 PAGES

100 PAGES
Published by Hesperus Press Limited
4 Rickett Street, London SW6 1RU
www.hesperuspress.com

'Rappaccini's Daughter' first published in 1844 in *Democratic Review*; 'Young Goodman Brown' first published in 1835 in *New England Magazine*; 'A Select Party' first published in 1844 in *Democratic Review* – the three stories first appeared together in the collection *Mosses from an Old Manse* in 1846

This edition first published by Hesperus Press Limited, 2003

Foreword © Simon Schama, 2003

Designed and typeset by Fraser Muggeridge
Printed in the United Arab Emirates by Oriental Press

ISBN: 1-84391-035-7

CONTENTS

FOREWORD

The most improbable compliment to Nathaniel Hawthorne was paid by Ian Fleming when he recreated the motif of a poisoned garden from 'Rappaccini's Daughter' in what is probably the best, and certainly the weirdest, of his Bond novels, *You Only Live Twice*. Set in Japan – and utterly unlike the predictable movie confection of bath-house titillation and exploding aluminium – Fleming's novel has the reclusive villain, Ernst Stavro Blofeld, make himself over as benefactor to the suicidally inclined and terminally ill who come to the garden to fade over and out amidst toxic blossoms. Wrong-footed by this surprising turn, Bond comes over all morally woozy, and is last spied paddling off into the Sea of Japan with his pearl-girl, in a Zen-like trance of cosmic wow.

Hawthorne would have loved this. Although most readers, in Britain especially, will know him principally for *The Scarlet Letter* (which sat unread on my father's shelf of 'Classics' until one dark November day I started reading it with goggle-eyed disbelief), and so think of its author as the epitome of New England austerity and demon-driven repression, he was, in fact, the most luxuriant of the seed-bed sowers of American literature. Though he often shrank snail-like into stay-at-home furtiveness, the town which made him – Salem, Massachusetts – (as any visitor can still see,) faces the dark, windy ocean, and it was this that Hawthorne would stare at when he worked in its Custom House from 1846–9. Such inward/outward paradox was to be at the heart of his creativity. Unlike his friend Melville who did go venturing over the seas,

Hawthorne was often stuck on its anxious verge; though the explorations he would undertake would be the perilous roadsteads of the human psyche.

Most of the heroic figures of the formative age of American letters confound the clichés and stereotypes which European visitors to the United States were quick to apply to the young Republic. Captain Marryat and Frances Trollope (Anthony's mother) concluded from their largely dispiriting experiences that the Americans were, by and large, a soulless, relentlessly practical people with a distinct deficit on the imaginative side – consumed by devotions to the Almighty dollar and incapable of rising above a raw and unforgiving utilitarianism. But none of the masters of ante-bellum America (not even James Fenimore Cooper) remotely corresponded to this identikit image of matter-of-fact plainness. What Poe, Melville and Hawthorne all shared was precisely a resistance to the commonplace and the prosaic, and the capacity to translate the *apparently* ordinary into moral epics and allegories of profound and often tragic consequence. They were all romancers, metaphysicals, dabblers in literary alchemy determined to spin gossamer filigree out of the apparently unpromising flint of American life. And for a country founded on the repudiation of history, they were all, of course, obsessed with the weight of the past.

Nor could the chosen diction of the American have been further from the socially diagnostic wit of Jane Austen or the stuffed-pudding plenitude of the young Dickens. To the modern reader, the high-pitched, declamatory, self-consciously ornate prose of Hawthorne in particular, often sounds on the edge of histrionics and makes his writing either awkwardly archaic or shockingly modern. The characters in 'Rappaccini's Daughter' are much given to exclaiming 'Perchance' or 'Methinks', but the stagey vocalising, far from reducing the milieu into a poor pseudo-Scottian pastiche, actually gives them a strange floating temporality, halfway between myth and social reality. In any event, this language could never be confused with any sort of importation of the English novel. It was something utterly new in the world, this Yankee lit-lingo – scriptural, oracular, densely and passionately wrought. And in Hawthorne's case it seems to bear little fruit. Though Henry James deeply admired the psychological intensity of Hawthorne's work, his own writing travelled on from it with the haste of a man fleeing sultry discomforts for cooler climes.

If Melville (as his friend Hawthorne ruefully acknowledged) was incomparably the greatest of these literary re-inventors, and Poe the most celebrated in his day (until Mark Twain came along), then the author of 'Rappaccini's Daughter' was surely the most creatively tormented, an unhealed casualty in the old tug of war between Puritanism and sensuality. 'The spirit of my Puritan ancestors was mighty on me,' he confessed, as well he might since a great-grandfather Hathorne had been one of the judges in the Salem witch trials, and another had been a ferocious whipper of Quakers. The classic Yankee conflict between small-town claustrophobia and compulsive sea-roving played itself out in Hawthorne's own family. His father, also called Nathaniel, died of yellow fever in Surinam when Nathaniel was just four, a loss that may have contributed to his later obsessions with often rather ominous father-figures (of whom Dr Rappaccini is the most alarming of all). Draped in widow's weeds, his mother moved the boy and his two sisters into an upper storey of her own Manning family's big house in Salem, populated by five uncles and three aunts, and for which she paid rent to the rest of the family. Nathaniel grew up very close to his two sisters, one older, one younger, but otherwise a conspicuously shy boy, grey-eyed, black-haired, and much given to solitary walks.

In 1821 he was sent to Bowdoin College in Maine (a state where the Mannings had property), and the crust of willed autonomy cracked a bit in a school where the student body numbered just one hundred and thirty-eight, and where his friends included the future President Franklin Pierce. His determination to somehow lead his own life was signalled by a change of name from Hathorne to Hawthorne, but the eccentric, tentative addition of the 'w' also suggested just how insecure he still was about his destiny. His uncle, Robert Manning, wanted him to join the successful family stagecoach business. Nathaniel longed to be a writer, but confessed that even as he did so he felt the burden of ancestral disapproval glowering at him for being a mere 'teller of stories'. So for the twelve years after his graduation in 1825, he did nothing at all very much, except live in the great house at Salem, read, write, dream, walk, and be quite unhappy quite a lot of the time. On those walks he must have heard the 'Hawthorne' voice first make utterance in its sinuous oddity, yet he still seemed hard-pressed to get it into writing. In the preface to another story, 'The Snow Image', he described this sense of occlusion as he 'sat down by the wayside of life, like a man under enchantment, and a shrubbery sprung up around me, and the bushes grew to be saplings, and the saplings became trees, until no exit appeared possible through the tangling depths of my obscurity'.

In 1828 a novel, *Fanshawe*, was published. It owed altogether too much to Scott and was a fiasco which stung its author so badly that a story claims he sought out all the copies he could find to have them burnt. At the age of thirty-two, in an effort to break out of his suffocating isolation (for there was another modestly gregarious Nat who, on trips around New England, would chat to travellers and entertain their own yarns), Hawthorne moved to Boston. For five hundred dollars (not always paid) he edited and wrote most of the content of *The American Magazine of Useful and Entertaining Knowledge* before it went bankrupt through no fault of his. For another hundred he wrote, together with his sister Elizabeth, *Peter Parley's Universal History on the Basis of Geography*, a children's book which over time sold very well indeed. Although this kind of production seemed a step down from being New England's answer to Walter Scott, the immersion in popular genres actually served Hawthorne well in the development of his own distinctive voice. When *Twice-Told Tales* appeared in 1837 (secretly financed by his old Bowdoin friend Horatio Bridge), it was as though Hawthorne had become a 'finder' of stories which were immanent in the ancestral culture of America itself. The 'writer' who had become locked up when faced with an utterly blank sheet, was now somewhat released by the conceit that he merely discovered what had been lying there all along, even in this newest of western cultures. In a country addicted to novelty and invention he was proceeding to supply an instant lore of allegory, myth and fable.

Twice-Told Tales was a critical success which finally made Hawthorne a name. But it did not bring him enough money to be an independent writer. In 1839 he took a job as Gauger of Salt and Coal, a diurnal round so prosaic that it perhaps fed his increasing flirtation with the fantastic. But his time in Boston, very much the self-proclaimed 'Athens' of Yankee culture, did certainly loosen up Hawthorne's fretful tightness. He began seeing women other than his sisters, and women, moreover, who were at the forefront of social and educational reform – like Margaret Fuller, feminist and abolitionist, and Elizabeth Peabody, who founded the kindergarten movement in America. And some time in 1837 he began to pay court, with some ardour, to Sophia Peabody, Elizabeth's sister. Before they married, in 1842, there was another break-out on Hawthorne's part when he invested fifteen hundred dollars in the Transcendentalist-socialist commune of Brook Farm at West Roxbury, just outside Boston. As one of the original settlers in 1841, Hawthorne did his bit, milking cows and raking hay. Though his appetite for rustic utopianism lasted just a few months, the experience supplied rich material for a later novel, the extraordinary tour de force, *The Blithedale Romance*.

Sophia and Nathaniel married in 1842 and moved to Concord, west of Boston, where they rented, from Ralph Waldo Emerson's family, The Old Manse, close by the river and the Old North Bridge where a bloody skirmish had taken place between British troops and local militia on 19th April 1775, the revolution's baptism of fire. In perfectly bucolic and culturally congenial surroundings, Hawthorne's imagination took flight and his pen dashed over the page, producing twenty-one stories, many of which, including 'Rappaccini's Daughter', would be collected in 1846 as *Mosses from an Old Manse*. In the preface to the book (written back in Salem after the Hawthornes had been evicted by Ralph Waldo Emerson for back rent), Nathaniel wrote with exquisite beauty and feeling of the place as a shrine of half-ruined memories and mute witnesses; not just redcoats and minutemen, but also the Indians who had occupied the land before the affray. In the pretty yard around the house Hawthorne communed with a world of happy vegetation. (Emerson may have turned out to be an unforgiving landlord, but he had after all written the greatest of his essays, *Nature*, in the attic-study of the Manse.) Instead of ideological hoeing at Brook Farm, Hawthorne wanders, both in pen and person, through the old orchard, planted by a clergyman in his old age 'when the neighbours laughed at the hoary-headed man for planting trees from which he could have no prospect of gathering fruit… But the old minister, before reaching his patriarchal age of ninety, ate the apples from this orchard during many years, and added silver and gold to his annual stipend, by disposing of the superfluity. It is pleasant to think of him walking among the trees in the quiet afternoons of early autumn, and picking up here and there a windfall; while he observes how heavily the branches are weighed down, and computes the number of empty flour-barrels that will be filled by their burden.

He loved each tree, doubtless as if it had been his own child. An orchard has a relation to mankind, and readily connects itself with matters of the heart.'

His Calvinist imagination, quick to conjure doom, and possibly the looming shadow of debt which would end in his expulsion from the paradise garden at Concord, provoked Hawthorne to create something very like its obverse: namely a garden of death. The conceit of vegetable sympathy, of someone who could love each tree 'as if it had been his own child' was pushed further and further, and then flipped over altogether into a parable about malevolent possession – in this case the malignant fate determined for his daughter by the arch-devotee of science, Dr Rappaccini. Beatrice, the toxic beauty, calls the purple-flowering plant at the centre of the sinister garden her 'sister', and the story turns on her symbiotic relationship with a habitat grown to kill.

As with all Hawthorne's fantastic stories, and especially those written for *Mosses* like 'The Bosom Serpent' or 'The Birth-Mark' (in which a husband becomes so obsessed with his otherwise ravishing wife's single blemish that he resolves to remove it at whatever cost), there is more going on here than an exercise in the ornamental grotesque. No visit from Dr Freud is needed to recognise that the devouring snake lurking deep in the body of the hysteric in 'The Bosom Serpent' is not just the 'egotism' of the longer title of the story, but guilt for auto-erotic naughtiness. But in his confessional mode, Hawthorne needed a modicum of disguise. He was not, as he said in the preface to *Mosses*, 'one of those supremely hospitable people who serve up their own hearts, delicately fried, with brain sauce as a titbit for their beloved public'. So he positively enjoyed draping what is, in fact, a chilling allegory of paternal possessiveness and pseudo-scientific fanaticism, in the gaudy fabric of a 'romance', just as the author pretends, in his pseudo-preface, to have discovered it among the works of 'M. de l'Aubépine' (French for 'hawthorn'). This slightly arch disguise of a French alter ego allows Hawthorne to pretend that the story is another of his 'finds', and so invests it with a kind of immemorial halo – a cautionary fable from ancestral wisdom.

The Padua of the setting belongs more to the repertoire of theatre (like the Shakespearean play or the romantic opera) or perhaps to Hawthorne's reading of Stendhal's *The Charterhouse of Parma* or even Manzoni, than to any sort of serious background research, much less immediate experience. Hawthorne would not get to Europe until 1853 when he was appointed United States Consul to Liverpool by his old friend Pierce, now President. When Pierce failed to be re-elected, and Hawthorne thus lost the post, he decided to stay in England, and in 1858 finally took the long-postponed trip to Italy. But the Rappaccini Padua, written more than a decade before, has a cut-out cast of types: the mad scientist; his jealous rival, Dr Baglioni, who spills the goods; the ingenuous juvenile lead-narrator Giovanni; and the fated beauty, Beatrice, whose every breath is a puff of pesticide.

Yet somehow – despite all the B-movie absurdity – the thing works, and works like a more benign version of the insidious Rappaccini spell: slowly, softly, irreversibly. (*Caveat lector* – do not read this book before going to sleep.) It works because, beneath all the flummery and phantasmagoria, the tentacular vines and the drooping purple 'gems', 'M. de l'Aubépine', as usual, has uncovered something dark in the nature of human relations – in this case the instinct for parents, and perhaps especially fathers, to wish to grow their daughters in their own image and according to their own design, and, worse, to make sure that once grown those daughters are never capable of true biological (or in the Rappaccini case, horticultural) separation. That Hawthorne managed to do this at precisely the time he was settling down to a fairly happy family life, and in the very year that his daughter Una was born, can only be explained by using the story as preemptive therapy against the Darker Side; the painful sense of the evanescence of happiness; the fake shimmer of deadly beauty.

Hawthorne was, in fact, deeply interested in the ambiguities of the parent-child relationship. He would return to the subject again and again, for example in his reworking of the Midas myth, in which a daughter, Marygold (and thus another flower), is turned into the metal by her father's kiss, even as he devoted his life to accumulating treasure for her sake. And the experimental pedagogy which flourished in New England fascinated him, even as he never quite found his own version of the ideal system. In yet another of the family's peregrinations, Hawthorne rented the Wayside Cottage, also at Concord, from Bronson Alcott, the father of the author of *Little Women*, but also a famously difficult educator who created the alternative Temple School in Boston, and subjected his own family to a notoriously austere regime in which the mind definitely took preference over the body, even to the point of both the little women and the big going hungry. Hawthorne admired Alcott and insisted on home schooling for his own three children, somewhat perversely refusing to let them read until they were seven.

It is difficult, in fact, to reread 'Rappaccini's Daughter', with its portrait of a father ready to sacrifice his child to his intellectual egotism, and not be put in mind of something like Hawthorne's cruelly fluctuating mood swings about his own children. And because he was alternately fascinated and repelled by strong women, he may have been especially hard on his daughters, Una and Rose. Rose recalled her father's fury when she tried her own hand at writing, his face 'dark as a flight of prophetic birds'. But Una may have been her father's deepest source of love and anguish. After catching malaria from a mosquito bite in the Colosseum, she fell desperately ill and for many months seemed close to death. Both her mother and father nursed her constantly, taking her first back to England, then finally back to New England where she recovered somewhat, but incompletely. She developed some sort of neural disorder (perhaps from lingering encephalitis) which made Hawthorne, in desperation, call for the services of an 'electric witch' who administered a primitive form of shock treatment to the unfortunate girl.

'Rappaccini's Daughter' was of course written long before this sadness overcame the family. (Nathaniel was equally badly hit when his younger sister Louisa died in a steamboat accident on the Hudson.) But the story is a psychological document of Hawthorne's propensity to see girl-children as the sacrificial victims of their father's vanity, masquerading as the vocation of knowledge. There is something else lurking in this wonderfully nasty tale, of course: namely physical possessiveness. Rappaccini will only release Beatrice from her hermetic isolation from the world and from the carnal knowledge men will give her, once he has 'adapted' a suitor as biological propagator of his precious bloom. The fancy is so outlandish, yet the unsettling instinct hidden in the luxuriance of the poison garden so resolutely explored, that it is no wonder that, on reading this and other of his tales after his father had died in 1864, Julian Hawthorne wrote that he was 'unable to comprehend how a man such as I knew my father to have been could have written such books'.

– Simon Schama, 2003

Rappaccini's Daughter

We do not remember to have seen any translated specimens of the productions of M. de l'Aubépine[1] – a fact the less to be wondered at, as his very name is unknown to many of his own countrymen as well as to the student of foreign literature. As a writer, he seems to occupy an unfortunate position between the Transcendentalists (who, under one name or another, have their share in all the current literature of the world) and the great body of pen-and-ink men who address the intellect and sympathies of the multitude. If not too refined, at all events too remote, too shadowy, and insubstantial in his modes of development to suit the taste of the latter class, and yet too popular to satisfy the spiritual or metaphysical requisitions of the former, he must necessarily find himself without an audience, except here and there an individual or possibly an isolated clique. His writings, to do them justice, are not altogether destitute of fancy and originality; they might have won him greater reputation but for an inveterate love of allegory, which is apt to invest his plots and characters with the aspect of scenery and people in the clouds, and to steal away the human warmth out of his conceptions. His fictions are sometimes historical, sometimes of the present day, and sometimes, so far as can be discovered, have little or no reference either to time or space. In any case, he generally contents himself with a very slight embroidery of outward manners – the faintest possible counterfeit of real life – and endeavours to create an interest by some less obvious peculiarity of the subject. Occasionally a breath of Nature, a raindrop of pathos and tenderness, or a gleam of humour, will find its way into the midst of his fantastic imagery, and make us feel as if, after all, we were yet within *the limits of our native earth. We will only add to this very cursory notice that M. de l'Aubépine's productions, if the reader chance to take them in precisely the proper point of view, may amuse a leisure hour as well as those of a brighter man; if otherwise, they can hardly fail to look excessively like nonsense.*

Our author is voluminous – he continues to write and publish with as much praiseworthy and indefatigable prolixity as if his efforts were crowned with the brilliant success that so justly attends those of Eugène Sue[2]. *His first appearance was by a collection of stories in a long series of volumes entitled* 'Contes deux fois racontées'. *The titles of some of his more recent works (we quote from memory) are as follows:* 'Le Voyage Céleste à Chemin de Fer', *3 tom., 1838;* 'Le nouveau Père Adam et la nouvelle Mère Eve', *2 tom., 1839;* 'Roderic; ou le Serpent à l'estomac', *2 tom., 1840;* 'Le Culte du Feu', *a folio volume of ponderous research into the religion and ritual of the old Persian Ghebers, published in 1841;* 'La Soirée du Château en Espagne', *1 tom., 8vo, 1842; and* 'L'Artiste du Beau; ou le Papillon Mécanique', *5 tom., 4to, 1843.*[3] *Our somewhat wearisome perusal of this startling catalogue of volumes has left behind it a certain personal affection and sympathy, though by no means admiration, for M. de l'Aubépine, and we would fain do the little in our power towards introducing him favourably to the American public. The ensuing tale is a translation of his* 'Beatrice; ou la Belle Empoisonneuse', *recently published in* 'La Revue Anti-Aristocratique'[4]. *This journal, edited by the Comte de Bearhaven*[5], *has for some years past led the defence of liberal principles and popular rights with a faithfulness and ability worthy of all praise.*

4

A young man named Giovanni Guasconti came, very long ago, from the more southern region of Italy to pursue his studies at the University of Padua. Giovanni, who had but a scanty supply of gold ducats in his pocket, took lodgings in a high and gloomy chamber of an old edifice which looked not unworthy to have been the palace of a Paduan noble, and which, in fact, exhibited over its entrance the armorial bearings of a family long since extinct. The young stranger, who was not unstudied in the great poem of his country, recollected that one of the ancestors of this family, and perhaps an occupant of this very mansion, had been pictured by Dante as a partaker of the immortal agonies of his Inferno. These reminiscences and associations, together with the tendency to heartbreak natural to a young man for the first time out of his native sphere, caused Giovanni to sigh heavily as he looked around the desolate and ill-furnished apartment.

'Holy Virgin, signor,' cried old dame Lisabetta, who, won by the youth's remarkable beauty of person, was kindly endeavouring to give the chamber a habitable air, 'what a sigh was that to come out of a young man's heart! Do you find this old mansion gloomy? For the love of heaven, then, put your head out of the window, and you will see as bright sunshine as you have left in Naples.'

Guasconti mechanically did as the old woman advised, but could not quite agree with her that the Lombard sunshine was as cheerful as that of southern Italy. Such as it was, however, it fell upon a garden beneath the window, and expended its fostering influences on a variety of plants which seemed to have been cultivated with exceeding care.

'Does this garden belong to the house?' asked Giovanni.

'Heaven forbid, signor! – unless it were fruitful of better pot-herbs than any that grow there now,' answered old Lisabetta. 'No; that garden is cultivated by the own hands of Signor Giacomo Rappaccini, the famous doctor who, I warrant him, has been heard of as far as Naples. It is said he distils these plants into medicines that are as potent as a charm. Oftentimes you may see the signor doctor at work, and perchance the signora his daughter, too, gathering the strange flowers that grow in the garden.'

The old woman had now done what she could for the aspect of the chamber, and, commending the young man to the protection of the saints, took her departure.

Giovanni still found no better occupation than to look down into the garden beneath his window. From its appearance he judged it to be one of those botanic gardens which were of earlier date in Padua than elsewhere in Italy, or in the world. Or, not improbably, it might once have been the pleasure place of an opulent family, for there was the ruin of a marble fountain in the centre, sculptured with rare art, but so woefully shattered that it was impossible to trace the original design from the chaos of remaining fragments. The water, however, continued to gush and sparkle into the sunbeams as cheerfully as ever. A little gurgling sound ascended to the young man's window, and made him feel as if a fountain were an immortal spirit that sung its song unceasingly and without heeding the vicissitudes around it, while one century embodied it in marble, and another scattered the perishable garniture on the soil. All about the pool into which the water subsided grew various plants that seemed to require a plentiful supply of moisture for the nourishment of gigantic leaves and, in some instances, flowers gorgeously magnificent. There was one shrub in particular, set in a marble vase in the midst of the pool, that bore a profusion of purple blossoms, each of which had the lustre and richness of a gem, and the whole together made a show so resplendent that it seemed enough to illuminate the garden, even had there been no sunshine. Every portion of the soil was peopled with plants and herbs, which, if less beautiful, still bore tokens of assiduous care, as if all had their individual virtues, known to the scientific mind that fostered them. Some were placed in urns, rich with old carving, and others in common garden-pots; some crept serpent-like along the ground, or climbed on high, using whatever means of ascent was offered them. One plant had wreathed itself round a statue of Vertumnus[6], which was thus quite veiled and shrouded in a drapery of hanging foliage, so happily arranged that it might have served a sculptor for a study.

While Giovanni stood at the window, he heard a rustling behind a screen of leaves, and became aware that a person was at work in the garden. His figure soon emerged into view, and showed itself to be that of no common labourer, but a tall, emaciated, sallow, and sickly looking man, dressed in a scholar's garb of black. He was beyond the middle term of life, with grey hair, a thin grey beard, and a face singularly marked with intellect and cultivation, but which could never, even in his more youthful days, have expressed much warmth of heart.

Nothing could exceed the intentness with which this

scientific gardener examined every shrub which grew in his path: it seemed as if he was looking into their inmost nature, making observations in regard to their creative essence, and discovering why one leaf grew in this shape, and another in that, and wherefore such and such flowers differed among themselves in hue and perfume. Nevertheless, in spite of the deep intelligence on his part, there was no approach to intimacy between himself and these vegetable existences. On the contrary, he avoided their actual touch, or the direct inhaling of their odours, with a caution that impressed Giovanni most disagreeably; for the man's demeanour was that of one walking among malignant influences, such as savage beasts, or deadly snakes, or evil spirits, which, should he allow them one moment of license, would wreak upon him some terrible fatality. It was strangely frightful to the young man's imagination to see this air of insecurity in a person cultivating a garden, that most simple and innocent of human toils, and which had been alike the joy and labour of the unfallen parents of the race. Was this garden, then, the Eden of the present world? – and this man, with such a perception of harm in what his own hands caused to grow, was he the Adam?

The distrustful gardener, while plucking away the dead leaves or pruning the too luxuriant growth of the shrubs, defended his hands with a pair of thick gloves. Nor were these his only armour. When, in his walk through the garden, he came to the magnificent plant that hung its purple gems beside the marble fountain, he placed a kind of mask over his mouth and nostrils, as if all this beauty did but conceal a deadlier malice. But finding his task still too dangerous, he drew back, removed the mask, and called loudly, but in the infirm voice of a person affected with inward disease:

'Beatrice! – Beatrice!'

'Here am I, my father! What would you?' cried a rich and youthful voice from the window of the opposite house; a voice as rich as a tropical sunset, and which made Giovanni, though he knew not why, think of deep hues of purple or crimson, and of perfumes heavily delectable. 'Are you in the garden?'

'Yes, Beatrice,' answered the gardener, 'and I need your help.'

Soon there emerged from under a sculptured portal the figure of a young girl, arrayed with as much richness of taste as the most splendid of the flowers, beautiful as the day, and with a bloom so deep and vivid that one shade more would have been too much. She looked redundant with life, health, and energy; all of which attributes were bound down and compressed, as it were, and girdled tensely, in their luxuriance, by her virgin zone. Yet Giovanni's fancy must have grown morbid while he looked down into the garden, for the impression which the fair stranger made upon him was as if here were another flower, the human sister of those vegetable ones, as beautiful as they – more beautiful than the richest of them – but still to be touched only with a glove, nor to be approached without a mask. As Beatrice came down the garden path, it was observable that she handled and inhaled the odour of several of the plants which her father had most sedulously avoided.

'Here, Beatrice,' said the latter, 'see how many needful

offices require to be done to our chief treasure. Yet, shattered as I am, my life might pay the penalty of approaching it so closely as circumstances demand. Henceforth, I fear, this plant must be consigned to your sole charge.'

'And gladly will I undertake it,' cried again the rich tones of the young lady, as she bent towards the magnificent plant, and opened her arms as if to embrace it. 'Yes, my sister, my splendour, it shall be Beatrice's task to nurse and serve thee; and thou shalt reward her with thy kisses and perfumed breath, which to her is as the breath of life!'

Then, with all the tenderness in her manner that was so strikingly expressed in her words, she busied herself with such attentions as the plant seemed to require; and Giovanni, at his lofty window, rubbed his eyes, and almost doubted whether it were a girl tending her favourite flower, or one sister performing the duties of affection to another. The scene soon terminated. Whether Dr Rappaccini had finished his labours in the garden, or that his watchful eye had caught the stranger's face, he now took his daughter's arm and retired. Night was already closing in; oppressive exhalations seemed to proceed from the plants and steal upwards past the open window; and Giovanni, closing the lattice, went to his couch and dreamt of a rich flower and beautiful girl. Flower and maiden were different and yet the same, and fraught with some strange peril in either shape.

But there is an influence in the light of morning that tends to rectify whatever errors of fancy, or even of judgement, we may have incurred during the sun's decline, or among the shadows of the night, or in the less wholesome glow of moonshine. Giovanni's first movement on starting from sleep was to throw open the window and gaze down into the garden which his dreams had made so fertile of mysteries. He was surprised, and a little ashamed, to find how real and matter-of-fact an affair it proved to be, in the first rays of the sun, which gilded the dewdrops that hung upon leaf and blossom, and, while giving a brighter beauty to each rare flower, brought everything within the limits of ordinary experience. The young man rejoiced that, in the heart of the barren city, he had the privilege of overlooking this spot of lovely and luxuriant vegetation. It would serve, he said to himself, as a symbolic language to keep him in communion with Nature. Neither the sickly and thought-worn Dr Giacomo Rappaccini, it is true, nor his brilliant daughter were now visible, so that Giovanni could not determine how much of the singularity which he attributed to both was due to their own qualities, and how much to his wonder-working fancy. But he was inclined to take a most rational view of the whole matter.

In the course of the day, he paid his respects to Signor Pietro Baglioni, Professor of Medicine in the University, a physician of eminent repute, to whom Giovanni had brought a letter of introduction. The professor was an elderly personage, apparently of genial nature, and habits that might almost be called jovial; he kept the young man to dinner, and made himself very agreeable by the freedom and liveliness of his conversation, especially when warmed by a flask or two of Tuscan wine. Giovanni, conceiving that men of science, inhabitants of the same city, must needs be on familiar terms with one another, took an opportunity to mention the name of Dr Rappaccini. But the professor did not respond with so much cordiality as he had anticipated.

'Ill would it become a teacher of the divine art of medicine,' said Professor Pietro Baglioni, in answer to a question of Giovanni, 'to withhold due and well-considered praise of a physician so eminently skilled as Rappaccini. But, on the other hand, I should answer it but scantily to my conscience were I to permit a worthy youth like yourself, Signor Giovanni, the son of an ancient friend, to imbibe erroneous ideas respecting a man who might hereafter chance to hold your life and death in his hands. The truth is, our worshipful Dr Rappaccini has as much science as any member of the faculty – with perhaps one single exception – in Padua, or all Italy. But there are certain grave objections to his professional character.'

'And what are they?' asked the young man.

'Has my friend Giovanni any disease of body or heart that he is so inquisitive about physicians?' said the professor, with a smile. 'But as for Rappaccini, it is said of him – and I, who know the man well, can answer for its truth – that he cares infinitely more for science than for mankind. His patients are interesting to him only as subjects for some new experiment. He would sacrifice human life, his own among the rest, or whatever else was dearest to him, for the sake of adding so much as a grain of mustard seed to the great heap of his accumulated knowledge.'

'Methinks he is an awful man, indeed,' remarked Guasconti, mentally recalling the cold and purely intellectual aspect of Rappaccini. 'And yet, worshipful professor, is it not a noble spirit? Are there many men capable of so spiritual a love of science?'

'God forbid,' answered the professor, somewhat testily – 'at least, unless they take sounder views of the healing art than those adopted by Rappaccini. It is his theory that all medicinal virtues are comprised within those substances which we term vegetable poisons. These he cultivates with his own hands, and is said even to have produced new varieties of poison, more horribly deleterious than Nature, without the assistance of this learned person, would ever have plagued the world withal. That the signor doctor does less mischief than might be expected with such dangerous substances is undeniable. Now and then, it must be owned, he has effected – or seemed to effect – a marvellous cure. But, to tell you my private mind, Signor Giovanni, he should receive little credit for such instances of success – they being probably the work of chance – but should be held strictly accountable for his failures, which may justly be considered his own work.'

The youth might have taken Baglioni's opinions with many grains of allowance had he known that there was a professional warfare of long continuance between him and Dr Rappaccini, in which the latter was generally thought to have gained the advantage. If the reader be inclined to judge for himself, we refer him to certain black-letter tracts on both sides, preserved in the medical department of the University of Padua.

'I know not, most learned professor,' returned Giovanni, after musing on what had been said of Rappaccini's exclusive zeal for science, 'I know not how dearly this physician may love his art, but surely there is one object more dear to him. He has a daughter.'

'Aha!' cried the professor, with a laugh. 'So now our friend Giovanni's secret is out. You have heard of this daughter, whom all the young men in Padua are wild about, though not half a dozen have ever had the good hap to see her face. I know little of the Signora Beatrice, save that Rappaccini is said to have instructed her deeply in his science, and that, young and beautiful as fame reports her, she is already qualified to fill a professor's chair. Perchance her father destines her for mine! Other absurd rumours there be, not worth talking about or listening to. So now, Signor Giovanni, drink off your glass of Lacryma.'

Guasconti returned to his lodgings somewhat heated with the wine he had quaffed, and which caused his brain to swim with strange fantasies in reference to Dr Rappaccini and the beautiful Beatrice. On his way, happening to pass by a florist's, he bought a fresh bouquet of flowers.

Ascending to his chamber, he seated himself near the window, but within the shadow thrown by the depth of the wall, so that he could look down into the garden with little risk of being discovered. All beneath his eye was a solitude. The strange plants were basking in the sunshine, and now and then nodding gently to one another, as if in acknowledgement of sympathy and kindred. In the midst, by the shattered fountain, grew the magnificent shrub, with its purple gems clustering all over it – they glowed in the air, and gleamed back again out of the depths of the pool, which thus seemed to overflow with coloured radiance from the rich reflection that was steeped in it. At first, as we have said, the garden was a solitude. Soon, however, as Giovanni had half-hoped, half-feared, would be the case, a figure appeared beneath the antique sculptured portal, and came down between the rows of plants, inhaling their various perfumes, as if she were one of those beings of old classic fable that lived upon sweet odours. On again beholding Beatrice, the young man was even startled to perceive how much her beauty exceeded his recollection of it; so brilliant, so vivid in its character, that she glowed amid the sunlight, and, as Giovanni whispered to himself, positively illuminated the more shadowy intervals of the garden path. Her face being now more revealed than on the former occasion, he was struck by its expression of simplicity and sweetness – qualities that had not entered into his idea of her character, and which made him ask anew what manner of mortal she might be. Nor did he fail again to observe, or imagine, an analogy between the beautiful girl and the gorgeous shrub that hung its gemlike flowers over the fountain; a resemblance which Beatrice seemed to have indulged a fantastic humour in heightening, both by the arrangement of her dress and the selection of its hues.

Approaching the shrub, she threw open her arms, as with a passionate ardour, and drew its branches into an intimate embrace – so intimate, that her features were hidden in its leafy bosom, and her glistening ringlets all intermingled with the flowers.

'Give me thy breath, my sister,' exclaimed Beatrice, 'for I am faint with common air! And give me this flower of thine, which I separate with gentlest fingers from the stem, and place it close beside my heart.'

With these words, the beautiful daughter of Rappaccini

plucked one of the richest blossoms of the shrub, and was about to fasten it in her bosom. But now, unless Giovanni's draughts of wine had bewildered his senses, a singular incident occurred. A small orange-coloured reptile, of the lizard or chameleon species, chanced to be creeping along the path, just at the feet of Beatrice. It appeared to Giovanni – but at the distance from which he gazed he could scarcely have seen anything so minute – it appeared to him, however, that a drop or two of moisture from the broken stem of the flower descended upon the lizard's head. For an instant the reptile contorted itself violently, and then lay motionless in the sunshine. Beatrice observed this remarkable phenomenon, and crossed herself, sadly, but without surprise; nor did she therefore hesitate to arrange the fatal flower in her bosom. There it blushed, and almost glimmered with the dazzling effect of a precious stone, adding to her dress and aspect the one appropriate charm, which nothing else in the world could have supplied. But Giovanni, out of the shadow of his window, bent forward and shrank back, and murmured and trembled.

'Am I awake? Have I my senses?' said he to himself. 'What is this being? – beautiful, shall I call her? – or inexpressibly terrible?'

Beatrice now strayed carelessly through the garden, approaching closer beneath Giovanni's window so that he was compelled to thrust his head quite out of its concealment in order to gratify the intense and painful curiosity which she excited. At this moment there came a beautiful insect over the garden wall; it had perhaps wandered through the city and found no flowers nor verdure among those antique haunts of men, until the heavy perfumes of Dr Rappaccini's shrubs had lured it from afar. Without alighting on the flowers, this winged brightness seemed to be attracted by Beatrice, and lingered in the air and fluttered about her head. Now here it could not be but that Giovanni Guasconti's eyes deceived him. Be that as it might, he fancied that while Beatrice was gazing at the insect with childish delight, it grew faint and fell at her feet – its bright wings shivered; it was dead – from no cause that he could discern, unless it were the atmosphere of her breath. Again Beatrice crossed herself and sighed heavily as she bent over the dead insect.

An impulsive movement of Giovanni drew her eyes to the window. There she beheld the beautiful head of the young man – rather a Grecian than an Italian head, with fair, regular features, and a glistening of gold among his ringlets – gazing down upon her like a being that hovered in mid-air. Scarcely knowing what he did, Giovanni threw down the bouquet which he had hitherto held in his hand.

'Signora,' said he, 'there are pure and healthful flowers. Wear them for the sake of Giovanni Guasconti!'

'Thanks, signor,' replied Beatrice, with her rich voice that came forth as it were like a gush of music; and with a mirthful expression half-childish and half-womanlike. 'I accept your gift, and would fain recompense it with this precious purple flower; but if I toss it into the air, it will not reach you. So Signor Guasconti must even content himself with my thanks.'

She lifted the bouquet from the ground, and then as if inwardly ashamed at having stepped aside from her maidenly reserve to respond to a stranger's greeting, passed swiftly homeward through the garden. But, few as the moments were, it seemed to Giovanni when she was on the point of vanishing beneath the sculptured portal, that his beautiful bouquet was already beginning to wither in her grasp. It was an idle thought; there could be no possibility of distinguishing a faded flower from a fresh one at so great a distance.

For many days after this incident, the young man avoided the window that looked into Dr Rappaccini's garden, as if something ugly and monstrous would have blasted his eyesight had he been betrayed into a glance. He felt conscious of having put himself, to a certain extent, within the influence of an unintelligible power, by the communication which he had opened with Beatrice. The wisest course would have been, if his heart were in any real danger, to quit his lodgings and Padua itself, at once; the next wiser, to have accustomed himself, as far as possible, to the familiar and daylight view of Beatrice, thus bringing her rigidly and systematically within the limits of ordinary experience. Least of all, while avoiding her sight, should Giovanni have remained so near this extraordinary being that the proximity and possibility even of intercourse should give a kind of substance and reality to the wild vagaries which his imagination ran riot continually in producing. Guasconti had not a deep heart – or at all events, its depths were not sounded now – but he had a quick fancy, and an ardent southern temperament which rose every instant to a higher fever pitch. Whether or no Beatrice possessed those terrible attributes – that fatal breath – the affinity with those so beautiful and deadly flowers – which were indicated by what Giovanni had witnessed, she had at least instilled a fierce and subtle poison into his system. It was not love, although her rich beauty was a madness to him; nor horror, even while he fancied her spirit to be imbued with the same baneful essence that seemed to pervade her physical frame; but a wild offspring of both love and horror that had each parent in it, and burned like one and shivered like the other. Giovanni knew not what to dread; still less did he know what to hope; yet hope and dread kept a continual warfare in his breast, alternately vanquishing one another and starting up afresh to renew the contest. Blessed are all simple emotions, be they dark or bright! It is the lurid intermixture of the two that produces the illuminating blaze of the infernal regions.

Sometimes he endeavoured to assuage the fever of his spirit by a rapid walk through the streets of Padua, or beyond its gates; his footsteps kept time with the throbbings of his brain so that the walk was apt to accelerate itself to a race. One day, he found himself arrested; his arm was seized by a portly personage who had turned back on recognising the young man, and expended much breath in overtaking him.

'Signor Giovanni! – stay, my young friend!' cried he. 'Have you forgotten me? That might well be the case, if I were as much altered as yourself.'

It was Baglioni, whom Giovanni had avoided ever since their first meeting, from a doubt that the professor's sagacity would look too deeply into his secrets. Endeavouring to recover himself, he stared forth wildly from his inner world into the outer one, and spoke like a man in a dream.

'Yes, I am Giovanni Guasconti. You are Professor Pietro Baglioni. Now let me pass!'

'Not yet – not yet, Signor Giovanni Guasconti,' said the professor, smiling, but at the same time scrutinising the youth with an earnest glance. 'What, did I grow up side by side with your father, and shall his son pass me like a stranger in these old streets of Padua? Stand still, Signor Giovanni, for we must have a word or two before we part.'

'Speedily, then, most worshipful professor, speedily!' said Giovanni, with feverish impatience. 'Does not your worship see that I am in haste?'

Now, while he was speaking, there came a man in black along the street, stooping and moving feebly, like a person in inferior health. His face was all overspread with a most sickly and sallow hue, but yet so pervaded with an expression of piercing and active intellect that an observer might easily have overlooked the merely physical attributes and have seen only this wonderful energy. As he passed, this person exchanged a cold and distant salutation with Baglioni, but fixed his eyes upon Giovanni with an intentness that seemed to bring out whatever was within him worthy of notice. Nevertheless, there was a peculiar quietness in the look, as if taking merely a speculative, not a human interest, in the young man.

'It is Dr Rappaccini!' whispered the professor, when the stranger had passed. '– Has he ever seen your face before?'

'Not that I know,' answered Giovanni, starting at the name.

'He *has* seen you! – he must have seen you!' said Baglioni, hastily. 'For some purpose or other, this man of science is making a study of you. I know that look of his! It is the same that coldly illuminates his face as he bends over a bird, a mouse, or a butterfly, which, in pursuance of some experiment, he has killed by the perfume of a flower; a look as deep as Nature itself, but without Nature's warmth of love. Signor Giovanni, I will stake my life upon it, you are the subject of one of Rappaccini's experiments!'

'Will you make a fool of me?' cried Giovanni, passionately. 'That, signor professor, were an untoward experiment.'

'Patience, patience!' replied the imperturbable professor. 'I tell thee, my poor Giovanni, that Rappaccini has a scientific interest in thee. Thou hast fallen into fearful hands! And the Signora Beatrice? What part does she act in this mystery?'

But Guasconti, finding Baglioni's pertinacity intolerable, here broke away, and was gone before the professor could again seize his arm. He looked after the young man intently, and shook his head.

'This must not be,' said Baglioni to himself. 'The youth is the son of my old friend, and shall not come to any harm from which the arcana of medical science can preserve him. Besides, it is too insufferable an impertinence in Rappaccini thus to snatch the lad out of my own hands, as I may say, and make use of him for his infernal experiments. This daughter of his! It shall be looked to. Perchance, most learned Rappaccini, I may foil you where you little dream of it!'

Meanwhile, Giovanni had pursued a circuitous route, and at length found himself at the door of his lodgings. As he crossed the threshold, he was met by old Lisabetta, who smirked and smiled, and was evidently desirous to attract his attention; vainly, however, as the ebullition of his feelings had momentarily subsided into a cold and dull vacuity. He turned his eyes full upon the withered face that was puckering itself into a smile, but seemed to behold it not. The old dame, therefore, laid her grasp upon his cloak.

'Signor! Signor!' whispered she, still with a smile over the whole breadth of her visage so that it looked not unlike a grotesque carving in wood, darkened by centuries. 'Listen, signor! There is a private entrance into the garden!'

'What do you say?' exclaimed Giovanni, turning quickly about, as if an inanimate thing should start into feverish life. '– A private entrance into Dr Rappaccini's garden!'

'Hush! hush! – not so loud!' whispered Lisabetta, putting her hand over his mouth. 'Yes; into the worshipful doctor's garden where you may see all his fine shrubbery. Many a young man in Padua would give gold to be admitted among those flowers.'

Giovanni put a piece of gold into her hand.

'Show me the way,' said he.

A surmise, probably excited by his conversation with Baglioni, crossed his mind that this interposition of old Lisabetta might perchance be connected with the intrigue, whatever were its nature, in which the professor seemed to suppose that Dr Rappaccini was involving him. But such a suspicion, though it disturbed Giovanni, was inadequate to restrain him. The instant he was aware of the possibility of approaching Beatrice, it seemed an absolute necessity of his existence to do so. It mattered not whether she were angel or demon; he was irrevocably within her sphere, and must obey the law that whirled him onward, in ever lessening circles, towards a result which he did not attempt to foreshadow. And yet, strange to say, there came across him a sudden doubt whether this intense interest on his part were not delusory – whether it were really of so deep and positive a nature as to justify him in now thrusting himself into an incalculable position – whether it were not merely the fantasy of a young man's brain, only slightly, or not at all, connected with his heart!

He paused – hesitated – turned half about – but again went on. His withered guide led him along several obscure passages, and finally undid a door through which, as it was opened, there came the sight and sound of rustling leaves, with the broken sunshine glimmering among them. Giovanni stepped forth, and forcing himself through the entanglement of a shrub that wreathed its tendrils over the hidden entrance, he stood beneath his own window in the open area of Dr Rappaccini's garden.

How often is it the case that, when impossibilities have come to pass, and dreams have condensed their misty substance into tangible realities, we find ourselves calm, and even coldly self-possessed, amid circumstances which it would have been a delirium of joy or agony to anticipate! Fate delights to thwart us thus. Passion will choose his own time to rush upon the scene, and lingers sluggishly behind when an appropriate adjustment of events would seem to summon his appearance. So was it now with Giovanni. Day after day his pulses had throbbed with feverish blood at the improbable idea of an interview with Beatrice, and of standing with her, face to face, in this very garden, basking in the oriental sunshine of her beauty, and snatching from her full gaze the mystery which he deemed the riddle of his own existence. But now there was a singular and untimely equanimity within his breast. He threw a glance around the garden to discover if Beatrice or her father were present, and perceiving that he was alone, began a critical observation of the plants.

The aspect of one and all of them dissatisfied him; their gorgeousness seemed fierce, passionate, and even unnatural. There was hardly an individual shrub which a wanderer, straying by himself through a forest, would not have been startled to find growing wild, as if an unearthly face had glared at him out of the thicket. Several, also, would have shocked a delicate instinct by an appearance of artificialness, indicating that there had been such commixture, and, as it were, adultery of various vegetable species, that the production was no longer of God's making, but the monstrous offspring of man's depraved fancy, glowing with only an evil mockery of beauty. They were probably the result of experiment which, in one or two cases, had succeeded in mingling plants individually lovely into a compound possessing the questionable and ominous character that distinguished the whole growth of the garden. In fine, Giovanni recognised but two or three plants in the collection, and those of a kind that he well knew to be poisonous. While busy with these contemplations, he heard the rustling of a silken garment, and turning, beheld Beatrice emerging from beneath the sculptured portal.

Giovanni had not considered with himself what should be his deportment; whether he should apologise for his intrusion into the garden, or assume that he was there with the privity, at least, if not by the desire, of Dr Rappaccini or his daughter. But Beatrice's manner placed him at his ease, though leaving him still in doubt by what agency he had gained admittance. She came lightly along the path, and met him near the broken fountain. There was surprise in her face, but brightened by a simple and kind expression of pleasure.

'You are a connoisseur in flowers, signor,' said Beatrice, with a smile, alluding to the bouquet which he had flung her from the window. 'It is no marvel, therefore, if the sight of my father's rare collection has tempted you to take a nearer view. If he were here, he could tell you many strange and interesting facts as to the nature and habits of these shrubs, for he has spent a lifetime in such studies, and this garden is his world.'

'And yourself, lady,' observed Giovanni, 'if fame says true, you, likewise, are deeply skilled in the virtues indicated by these rich blossoms, and these spicy perfumes. Would you deign to be my instructress, I should prove an apter scholar than under Signor Rappaccini himself.'

'Are there such idle rumours?' asked Beatrice, with the music of a pleasant laugh. 'Do people say that I am skilled in my father's science of plants? What a jest is there! No; though I have grown up among these flowers, I know no more of them than their hues and perfume; and sometimes methinks I would fain rid myself of even that small knowledge. There are many flowers here, and those not the least brilliant, that shock and offend me when they meet my eye. But, pray, signor, do not believe these stories about my science. Believe nothing of me save what you see with your own eyes.'

'And must I believe all that I have seen with my own eyes?' asked Giovanni, pointedly, while the recollection of former scenes made him shrink. 'No, signora, you demand too little of me. Bid me believe nothing save what comes from your own lips.'

It would appear that Beatrice understood him. There came a deep flush to her cheek, but she looked full into Giovanni's eyes, and responded to his gaze of uneasy suspicion with a queen-like haughtiness.

'I do so bid you, signor!' she replied. 'Forget whatever you may have fancied in regard to me. If true to the outward senses, still it may be false in its essence. But the words of Beatrice Rappaccini's lips are true from the heart outward. Those you may believe!'

A fervour glowed in her whole aspect, and beamed upon Giovanni's consciousness like the light of truth itself. But while she spoke, there was a fragrance in the atmosphere around her, rich and delightful, though evanescent, yet which the young man, from an indefinable reluctance, scarcely dared to draw into his lungs. It might be the odour of the flowers. Could it be Beatrice's breath which thus embalmed her words with a strange richness, as if by steeping them in her heart? A faintness passed like a shadow over Giovanni, and flitted away; he seemed to gaze through the beautiful girl's eyes into her transparent soul, and felt no more doubt or fear.

The tinge of passion that had coloured Beatrice's manner vanished; she became gay, and appeared to derive a pure delight from her communion with the youth, not unlike what the maiden of a lonely island might have felt conversing with a voyager from the civilised world.

Evidently her experience of life had been confined within the limits of that garden. She talked now about matters as simple as the daylight or summer clouds, and now asked questions in reference to the city, or Giovanni's distant home, his friends, his mother, and his sisters – questions indicating such seclusion and such lack of familiarity with modes and forms that Giovanni responded as if to an infant. Her spirit gushed out before him like a fresh rill that was just catching its first glimpse of the sunlight, and wondering at the reflections of earth and sky which were flung into its bosom. There came thoughts, too, from a deep source, and fantasies of a gemlike brilliancy, as if diamonds and rubies sparkled upwards among the bubbles of the fountain. Ever and anon there gleamed across the young man's mind a sense of wonder that he should be walking side by side with the being who had so wrought upon his imagination, whom he had idealised in such hues of terror, in whom he had positively witnessed such manifestations of dreadful attributes – that he should be conversing with Beatrice like a brother, and should find her so human and so maiden-like. But such reflections were only momentary – the effect of her character was too real not to make itself familiar at once.

In this free intercourse they had strayed through the garden, and now, after many turns among its avenues, were come to the shattered fountain, beside which grew the magnificent shrub with its treasury of glowing blossoms. A fragrance was diffused from it which Giovanni recognised as identical with that which he had attributed to Beatrice's breath, but incomparably more powerful. As her eyes fell upon it, Giovanni beheld her press her hand to her bosom, as if her heart were throbbing suddenly and painfully.

'For the first time in my life,' murmured she, addressing the shrub, 'I had forgotten thee!'

'I remember, signora,' said Giovanni, 'that you once promised to reward me with one of these living gems for the bouquet which I had the happy boldness to fling to your feet. Permit me now to pluck it as a memorial of this interview.'

He made a step towards the shrub with extended hand. But Beatrice darted forward, uttering a shriek that went through his heart like a dagger. She caught his hand, and drew it back with the whole force of her slender figure. Giovanni felt her touch thrilling through his fibres.

'Touch it not!' exclaimed she, in a voice of agony. 'Not for thy life! It is fatal!'

Then, hiding her face, she fled from him, and vanished beneath the sculptured portal. As Giovanni followed her with his eyes, he beheld the emaciated figure and pale intelligence of Dr Rappaccini who had been watching the scene – he knew not how long – within the shadow of the entrance.

No sooner was Guasconti alone in his chamber than the image of Beatrice came back to his passionate musings, invested with all the witchery that had been gathering around it ever since his first glimpse of her, and now likewise imbued with a tender warmth of girlish woman-hood. She was human; her nature was endowed with all gentle and feminine qualities; she was worthiest to be worshipped; she was capable, surely, on her part, of the height and heroism of love. Those tokens, which he had hitherto considered as proofs of a frightful peculiarity in her physical and moral system, were now either forgotten, or, by the subtle sophistry of passion, transmitted into a golden crown of enchantment, rendering Beatrice the more admirable, by so much as she was the more unique. Whatever had looked ugly was now beautiful; or, if incapable of such a change, it stole away and hid itself among those shapeless half-ideas which throng the dim region beyond the daylight of our perfect consciousness. Thus did he spend the night, nor fell asleep until the dawn had begun to awake the slumbering flowers in Dr Rappaccini's garden, whither his dreams doubtless led him. Up rose the sun in his due season, and flinging his beams upon the young man's eyelids, awoke him to a sense of pain. When thoroughly aroused, he became sensible of a burning and tingling agony in his hand – in his right hand – the very hand which Beatrice had grasped in her own when he was on the point of plucking one of the gemlike flowers. On the back of that hand there was now a purple print, like that of four small fingers, and the likeness of a slender thumb upon his wrist.

Oh, how stubbornly does love – or even that cunning semblance of love which flourishes in the imagination but strikes no depth of root into the heart – how stubbornly does it hold its faith, until the moment comes when it is doomed to vanish into thin mist! Giovanni wrapped a handkerchief about his hand, and wondered what evil thing had stung him, and soon forgot his pain in a reverie of Beatrice.

After the first interview, a second was in the inevitable course of what we call fate. A third; a fourth; and a meeting with Beatrice in the garden was no longer an incident in Giovanni's daily life, but the whole space in which he might be said to live, for the anticipation and memory of that ecstatic hour made up the remainder. Nor was it otherwise with the daughter of Rappaccini. She watched for the youth's appearance, and flew to his side with confidence as unreserved as if they had been playmates from early infancy – as if they were such playmates still. If, by any unwonted chance, he failed to come at the appointed moment, she stood beneath the window, and sent up the rich sweetness of her tones to float around him in his chamber, and echo and reverberate throughout his heart: 'Giovanni! Giovanni! Why tarriest thou? Come down!' And down he hastened into that Eden of poisonous flowers.

But, with all this intimate familiarity, there was still a reserve in Beatrice's demeanour so rigidly and invariably sustained that the idea of infringing it scarcely occurred to his imagination. By all appreciable signs, they loved; they had looked love with eyes that conveyed the holy secret from the depths of one soul into the depths of the other, as if it were too sacred to be whispered by the way; they had even spoken love in those gushes of passion when their spirits darted forth in articulated breath, like tongues of long-hidden flame; and yet there had been no seal of lips, no clasp of hands, nor any slightest caress such as love claims and hallows. He had never touched one of the gleaming ringlets of her hair; her garment – so marked was the physical barrier between them – had never been waved against him by a breeze. On the few occasions when Giovanni had seemed tempted to overstep the limit, Beatrice grew so sad, so stern, and withal wore such a look of desolate separation, shuddering at itself, that not a spoken word was requisite to repel him. At such times he was startled at the horrible suspicions that rose, monster-like, out of the caverns of his heart, and stared him in the face; his love grew thin and faint as the morning mist; his doubts alone had substance. But when Beatrice's face brightened again after the momentary shadow, she was transformed at once from the mysterious, questionable being whom he had watched with so much awe and horror; she was now the beautiful and unsophisticated girl whom he felt that his spirit knew with a certainty beyond all other knowledge.

A considerable time had now passed since Giovanni's last meeting with Baglioni. One morning, however, he was disagreeably surprised by a visit from the professor whom he had scarcely thought of for whole weeks and would willingly have forgotten still longer. Given up, as he had long been, to a pervading excitement, he could tolerate no companions, except upon condition of their perfect sympathy with his present state of feeling. Such sympathy was not to be expected from Professor Baglioni.

The visitor chatted carelessly for a few moments about the gossip of the city and the university, and then took up another topic.

'I have been reading an old classic author lately,' said he, 'and met with a story that strangely interested me. Possibly you may remember it. It is of an Indian prince who sent a beautiful woman as a present to Alexander the Great. She was as lovely as the dawn, and gorgeous as the sunset; but what specially distinguished her was a certain rich perfume in her breath – richer than a garden of Persian roses. Alexander – as was natural to a youthful conqueror – fell in love at first sight with this magnificent stranger. But a certain sage physician, happening to be present, discovered a terrible secret in regard to her.'

'And what was that?' asked Giovanni, turning his eyes downwards to avoid those of the professor.

'That this lovely woman,' continued Baglioni, with emphasis, 'had been nourished with poisons from her birth upwards, until her whole nature was so imbued with them that she herself had become the deadliest poison in existence. Poison was her element of life. With that rich perfume of her breath, she blasted the very air. Her love would have been poison! – her embrace death! Is not this a marvellous tale?'

'A childish fable,' answered Giovanni, nervously starting from his chair. 'I marvel how your worship finds time to read such nonsense among your graver studies.'

'By the by,' said the professor, looking uneasily about him, 'what singular fragrance is this in your apartment? Is it the perfume of your gloves? It is faint, but delicious, and yet, after all, by no means agreeable. Were I to breathe it long, methinks it would make me ill. It is like the breath of a flower – but I see no flowers in the chamber.'

'Nor are there any,' replied Giovanni, who had turned pale as the professor spoke. 'Nor, I think, is there any fragrance, except in your worship's imagination. Odours, being a sort of element combined of the sensual and the spiritual, are apt to deceive us in this manner. The recollection of a perfume – the bare idea of it – may easily be mistaken for a present reality.'

'Aye, but my sober imagination does not often play such tricks,' said Baglioni; 'and were I to fancy any kind of odour, it would be that of some vile apothecary drug, wherewith my fingers are likely enough to be imbued. Our worshipful friend Rappaccini, as I have heard, tinctures his medicaments with odours richer than those of Arabia. Doubtless, likewise, the fair and learned Signora Beatrice would minister to her patients with draughts as sweet as a maiden's breath. But woe to him that sips them!'

Giovanni's face evinced many contending emotions. The tone in which the professor alluded to the pure and lovely daughter of Rappaccini was a torture to his soul; and yet, the intimation of a view of her character opposite to his own gave instantaneous distinctness to a thousand dim suspicions which now grinned at him like so many demons. But he strove hard to quell them, and to respond to Baglioni with a true lover's perfect faith.

'Signor professor,' said he, 'you were my father's friend – perchance, too, it is your purpose to act a friendly part towards his son. I would fain feel nothing towards you save respect and deference. But I pray you to observe, signor, that there is one subject on which we must not speak. You know not the Signora Beatrice. You cannot, therefore, estimate the wrong – the blasphemy, I may even say – that is offered to her character by a light or injurious word.'

'Giovanni! – my poor Giovanni!' answered the professor, with a calm expression of pity, 'I know this wretched girl far better than yourself. You shall hear the truth in respect to the poisoner Rappaccini, and his poisonous daughter. Yes; poisonous as she is beautiful! Listen, for even should you do violence to my grey hairs, it shall not silence me. That old fable of the Indian woman has become a truth by the deep and deadly science of Rappaccini, and in the person of the lovely Beatrice!'

Giovanni groaned and hid his face.

'Her father,' continued Baglioni, 'was not restrained by natural affection from offering up his child in this horrible manner as the victim of his insane zeal for science. For – let us do him justice – he is as true a man of science as ever distilled his own heart in an alembic. What, then, will be your fate? Beyond a doubt, you are selected as the material of some new experiment. Perhaps the result is to be death – perhaps a fate more awful still! Rappaccini, with what he calls the interest of science before his eyes, will hesitate at nothing.'

'It is a dream!' muttered Giovanni to himself. 'Surely it is a dream!'

'But,' resumed the professor, 'be of good cheer, son of my friend! It is not yet too late for the rescue. Possibly we may even succeed in bringing back this miserable child within the limits of ordinary nature from which her father's madness has estranged her. Behold this little silver vase! It was wrought by the hands of the renowned Benvenuto Cellini, and is well worthy to be a love-gift to the fairest dame in Italy. But its contents are invaluable. One little sip of this antidote would have rendered the most virulent poisons of the Borgias innocuous. Doubt not that it will be as efficacious against those of Rappaccini. Bestow the vase, and the precious liquid within it, on your Beatrice, and hopefully await the result.'

Baglioni laid a small, exquisitely wrought silver phial on the table, and withdrew, leaving what he had said to produce its effect upon the young man's mind.

'We will thwart Rappaccini yet!' thought he, chuckling to himself, as he descended the stairs. 'But, let us confess the truth of him, he is a wonderful man! – a wonderful man indeed! A vile empiric, however, in his practice, and therefore not to be tolerated by those who respect the good old rules of the medical profession!'

Throughout Giovanni's whole acquaintance with Beatrice, he had occasionally, as we have said, been haunted by dark surmises as to her character. Yet, so thoroughly had she made herself felt by him as a simple, natural, most affectionate and guileless creature, that the image now held up by Professor Baglioni looked as strange and incredible as if it were not in accordance with his own original conception. True, there were ugly recollections connected with his first glimpses of the beautiful girl; he could not quite forget the bouquet that withered in her grasp, and the insect that perished amid the sunny air by no ostensible agency save the fragrance of her breath. These incidents, however, dissolving in the pure light of her character, had no longer the efficacy of facts, but were acknowledged as mistaken fantasies by whatever testimony of the senses they might appear to be substantiated. There is something truer and more real than what we can see with the eyes and touch with the finger. On such better evidence had Giovanni founded his confidence in Beatrice, though rather by the necessary force of her high attributes than by any deep and generous faith on his part. But, now, his spirit was incapable of sustaining itself at the height to which the early enthusiasm of passion had exalted it; he fell down, grovelling among earthly doubts, and defiled therewith the pure whiteness of Beatrice's image. Not that he gave her up; he did but distrust. He resolved to institute some decisive test that should satisfy him, once and for all, whether there were those dreadful peculiarities in her physical nature which could not be supposed to exist without some corresponding monstrosity of soul. His eyes, gazing down afar, might have deceived him as to the lizard, the insect, and the flowers. But if he could witness, at the distance of a few paces, the sudden blight of one fresh and healthful flower in Beatrice's hand, there would be room for no further question. With this idea, he hastened to the florist's, and purchased a bouquet that was still gemmed with the morning dewdrops.

It was now the customary hour of his daily interview with Beatrice. Before descending into the garden, Giovanni failed not to look at his figure in the mirror – a vanity to be expected in a beautiful young man, yet, as displaying itself at that troubled and feverish moment, the token of a certain shallowness of feeling and insincerity of character. He did gaze, however, and said to himself that his features had never before possessed so rich a grace, nor his eyes such vivacity, nor his cheeks so warm a hue of superabundant life.

'At least,' thought he, 'her poison has not yet insinuated itself into my system. I am no flower to perish in her grasp!'

With that thought, he turned his eyes on the bouquet which he had never once laid aside from his hand. A thrill of indefinable horror shot through his frame on perceiving that those dewy flowers were already beginning to droop; they wore the aspect of things that had been fresh and lovely yesterday. Giovanni grew white as marble, and stood motionless before the mirror, staring at his own reflection there, as at the likeness of something frightful. He remembered Baglioni's remark about the fragrance that seemed to pervade the chamber. It must have been the poison in his breath! Then he shuddered – shuddered at himself! Recovering from his stupor, he began to watch, with curious eye, a spider that was busily at work hanging its web from the antique cornice of the apartment, crossing and re-crossing the artful system of interwoven lines, as vigorous and active a spider as ever dangled from an old ceiling. Giovanni bent towards the insect, and emitted a deep, long breath. The spider suddenly ceased its toil; the web vibrated with a tremor originating in the body of the small artisan. Again Giovanni sent forth a breath, deeper, longer, and imbued with a venomous feeling out of his heart; he knew not whether he were wicked or only desperate. The spider made a convulsive gripe with his limbs, and hung dead across the window.

'Accursed! Accursed!' muttered Giovanni, addressing himself. 'Hast thou grown so poisonous that this deadly insect perishes by thy breath?'

At that moment, a rich, sweet voice came floating up from the garden: 'Giovanni! Giovanni! It is past the hour! Why tarriest thou! Come down!'

'Yes,' muttered Giovanni, again. 'She is the only being whom my breath may not slay! Would that it might!'

He rushed down, and in an instant was standing before

the bright and loving eyes of Beatrice. A moment ago his wrath and despair had been so fierce that he could have desired nothing so much as to wither her by a glance. But with her actual presence there came influences which had too real an existence to be at once shaken off; recollections of the delicate and benign power of her feminine nature which had so often enveloped him in a religious calm; recollections of many a holy and passionate outgush of her heart when the pure fountain had been unsealed from its depths and made visible in its transparency to his mental eye; recollections which, had Giovanni known how to estimate them, would have assured him that all this ugly mystery was but an earthly illusion, and that, whatever mist of evil might seem to have gathered over her, the real Beatrice was a heavenly angel. Incapable as he was of such high faith, still her presence had not utterly lost its magic. Giovanni's rage was quelled into an aspect of sullen insensibility. Beatrice, with a quick spiritual sense, immediately felt that there was a gulf of blackness between them which neither he nor she could pass. They walked on together, sad and silent, and came thus to the marble fountain and to its pool of water on the ground, in the midst of which grew the shrub that bore gemlike blossoms. Giovanni was affrighted at the eager enjoyment – the appetite, as it were – with which he found himself inhaling the fragrance of the flowers.

'Beatrice,' asked he, abruptly, 'whence came this shrub!'

'My father created it,' answered she, with simplicity.

'Created it! created it!' repeated Giovanni. 'What mean you, Beatrice?'

'He is a man fearfully acquainted with the secrets of

nature,' replied Beatrice, 'and, at the hour when I first drew breath, this plant sprang from the soil, the offspring of his science, of his intellect, while I was but his earthly child. Approach it not!' continued she, observing with terror that Giovanni was drawing nearer to the shrub. 'It has qualities that you little dream of. But I, dearest Giovanni – I grew up and blossomed with the plant, and was nourished with its breath. It was my sister, and I loved it with a human affection; for – alas! hast thou not suspected it? – there was an awful doom.'

Here Giovanni frowned so darkly upon her that Beatrice paused and trembled. But her faith in his tenderness reassured her, and made her blush that she had doubted for an instant.

'There was an awful doom,' she continued, 'the effect of my father's fatal love of science, which estranged me from all society of my kind. Until Heaven sent thee, dearest Giovanni, Oh! how lonely was thy poor Beatrice!'

'Was it a hard doom?' asked Giovanni, fixing his eyes upon her.

'Only of late have I known how hard it was,' answered she, tenderly. 'Oh, yes; but my heart was torpid, and therefore quiet.'

Giovanni's rage broke forth from his sullen gloom like a lightning flash out of a dark cloud.

'Accursed one!' cried he, with venomous scorn and anger. 'And finding thy solitude wearisome, thou hast severed me, likewise, from all the warmth of life, and enticed me into thy region of unspeakable horror!'

'Giovanni!' exclaimed Beatrice, turning her large bright eyes upon his face. The force of his words had not found its way into her mind; she was merely thunderstruck.

'Yes, poisonous thing!' repeated Giovanni, beside himself with passion. 'Thou hast done it! Thou hast blasted me! Thou hast filled my veins with poison! Thou hast made me as hateful, as ugly, as loathsome and deadly a creature as thyself – a world's wonder of hideous monstrosity! Now – if our breath be happily as fatal to ourselves as to all others – let us join our lips in one kiss of unutterable hatred, and so die!'

'What has befallen me?' murmured Beatrice, with a low moan out of her heart. 'Holy Virgin pity me, a poor heartbroken child!'

'Thou! Dost thou pray?' cried Giovanni, still with the same fiendish scorn. 'Thy very prayers, as they come from thy lips, taint the atmosphere with death. Yes, yes; let us pray! Let us to church, and dip our fingers in the holy water at the portal! They that come after us will perish as by a pestilence. Let us sign crosses in the air! It will be scattering curses abroad in the likeness of holy symbols!'

'Giovanni,' said Beatrice, calmly, for her grief was beyond passion. 'Why dost thou join thyself with me thus in those terrible words? I, it is true, am the horrible thing thou namest me. But thou! – what hast thou to do, save with one other shudder at my hideous misery, to go forth out of the garden and mingle with thy race, and forget that there ever crawled on Earth such a monster as poor Beatrice?'

'Dost thou pretend ignorance?' asked Giovanni, scowling upon her. 'Behold! This power have I gained from the pure daughter of Rappaccini!'

There was a swarm of summer insects flitting through

the air in search of the food promised by the flower-odours of the fatal garden. They circled round Giovanni's head, and were evidently attracted towards him by the same influence which had drawn them, for an instant, within the sphere of several of the shrubs. He sent forth a breath among them, and smiled bitterly at Beatrice, as at least a score of the insects fell dead upon the ground.

'I see it! I see it!' shrieked Beatrice. 'It is my father's fatal science? No, no, Giovanni, it was not I! Never, never! I dreamt only to love thee, and be with thee a little time, and so to let thee pass away, leaving but thine image in mine heart. For, Giovanni – believe it – though my body be nourished with poison, my spirit is God's creature, and craves love as its daily food. But my father! – he has united us in this fearful sympathy. Yes; spurn me! – tread upon me! – kill me! Oh, what is death, after such words as thine? But it was not I! Not for a world of bliss would I have done it!'

Giovanni's passion had exhausted itself in its outburst from his lips. There now came across him a sense, mournful, and not without tenderness, of the intimate and peculiar relationship between Beatrice and himself. They stood, as it were, in an utter solitude, which would be made none the less solitary by the densest throng of human life. Ought not, then, the desert of humanity around them to press this insulated pair closer together? If they should be cruel to one another, who was there to be kind to them? Besides, thought Giovanni, might there not still be a hope of his returning within the limits of ordinary nature, and leading Beatrice – the redeemed Beatrice – by the hand? Oh, weak, and selfish, and unworthy spirit that could dream of an earthly union and earthly happiness as possible after such deep love had been so bitterly wronged as was Beatrice's love by Giovanni's blighting words! No, no; there could be no such hope. She must pass heavily, with that broken heart, across the borders of Time – she must bathe her hurts in some fount of Paradise, and forget her grief in the light of immortality – and there be well!

But Giovanni did not know it.

'Dear Beatrice,' said he, approaching her, while she shrank away, as always at his approach, but now with a different impulse. 'Dearest Beatrice, our fate is not yet so desperate. Behold! There is a medicine, potent, as a wise physician has assured me, and almost divine in its efficacy. It is composed of ingredients the most opposite to those by which thy awful father has brought this calamity upon thee and me. It is distilled of blessed herbs. Shall we not quaff it together, and thus be purified from evil?'

'Give it me!' said Beatrice, extending her hand to receive the little silver phial which Giovanni took from his bosom. She added, with a peculiar emphasis: 'I will drink – but do thou await the result.'

She put Baglioni's antidote to her lips, and, at the same moment, the figure of Rappaccini emerged from the portal, and came slowly towards the marble fountain. As he drew near, the pale man of science seemed to gaze with a triumphant expression at the beautiful youth and maiden, as might an artist who should spend his life in achieving a picture or a group of statuary, and finally be satisfied with his success. He paused, his bent form grew erect with conscious power, he spread out his hand over them, in the attitude of a father imploring a blessing upon his children. But those were the same hands that had thrown poison into the stream of their lives! Giovanni trembled. Beatrice shuddered very nervously, and pressed her hand upon her heart.

'My daughter,' said Rappaccini, 'thou art no longer lonely in the world! Pluck one of those precious gems from thy sister shrub, and bid thy bridegroom wear it in his bosom. It will not harm him now! My science, and the sympathy between thee and him, have so wrought within his system that he now stands apart from common men, as thou dost, daughter of my pride and triumph, from ordinary women. Pass on, then, through the world, most dear to one another, and dreadful to all besides!'

'My father,' said Beatrice, feebly – and still, as she spoke, she kept her hand upon her heart – 'wherefore didst thou inflict this miserable doom upon thy child?'

'Miserable!' exclaimed Rappaccini. 'What mean you, foolish girl? Dost thou deem it misery to be endowed with marvellous gifts, against which no power nor strength could avail an enemy? Misery, to be able to quell the mightiest with a breath? Misery, to be as terrible as thou art beautiful? Wouldst thou, then, have preferred the condition of a weak woman, exposed to all evil, and capable of none?'

'I would fain have been loved, not feared,' murmured Beatrice, sinking down upon the ground. 'But now it matters not. I am going, Father, where the evil, which thou hast striven to mingle with my being, will pass away like a dream – like the fragrance of these poisonous flowers which will no longer taint my breath among the flowers of Eden. Farewell, Giovanni! Thy words of hatred are like lead within my heart – but they, too, will fall away as I ascend. Oh, was there not, from the first, more poison in thy nature than in mine?'

To Beatrice – so radically had her earthly part been wrought upon by Rappaccini's skill – as poison had been life, so the powerful antidote was death. And thus the poor victim of man's ingenuity and of thwarted nature, and of the fatality that attends all such efforts of perverted wisdom, perished there, at the feet of her father and Giovanni. Just at that moment Professor Pietro Baglioni looked forth from the window, and called loudly, in a tone of triumph mixed with horror, to the thunderstricken man of science:

'Rappaccini! Rappaccini! And is this the upshot of your experiment?'

NOTES

1. Hawthorne often wrote under a pseudonym, and occasionally adopted the French name M. de l'Aubépine. *Aubépine* is the French word for Hawthorne.

2. French novelist Eugène Sue (1804–1914) was a prolific writer whose works often depicted the Parisian underworld.

3. The works cited are French translations of the titles of Hawthorne's own writings: '*Contes deux fois racontées*' refers to Hawthorne's collection, *Twice-Told Tales*, with the other works listed being 'The Celestial Railroad', 'The New Adam and Eve', 'Egotism; or The Bosom Serpent', 'Fire-worship' (the 'old Persian Ghebers' Hawthorne refers to were Fire-Worshippers) and 'The Artist of the Beautiful'. Hawthorne presumably chose these particular works for their pertinence to the ensuing story.

4. The story '*Beatrice; ou la Belle Empoisonneuse*' refers to 'Rappaccini's Daughter', and '*La Revue Anti-Aristocratique*' the *Democratic Review*, the journal where in fact 'Rappaccini's Daughter' first appeared.

5. Hawthorne humorously addressed John Louis O'Sullivan, founder of the *Democratic Review*, as the Comte de Bearhaven, a reference to an ancient title belonging to the O'Sullivan family.

6. Vertumnus was the Roman god of gardens and of the changing seasons.

Young Goodman Brown

Young Goodman Brown came forth at sunset into the street at Salem village, but put his head back, after crossing the threshold, to exchange a parting kiss with his young wife. And Faith, as the wife was aptly named, thrust her own pretty head into the street, letting the wind play with the pink ribbons of her cap, while she called to Goodman Brown.

'Dearest heart,' whispered she, softly and rather sadly, when her lips were close to his ear, 'prithee, put off your journey until sunrise, and sleep in your own bed tonight. A lone woman is troubled with such dreams and such thoughts that she's afeard of herself sometimes. Pray tarry with me this night, dear husband, of all nights in the year!'

'My love and my Faith,' replied young Goodman Brown, 'of all nights in the year, this one night must I tarry away from thee. My journey, as thou callest it, forth and back again, must needs be done 'twixt now and sunrise. What, my sweet, pretty wife, dost thou doubt me already, and we but three months married?'

'Then, God bless you!' said Faith, with the pink ribbons, 'and may you find all well when you come back.'

'Amen!' cried Goodman Brown. 'Say thy prayers, dear Faith, and go to bed at dusk, and no harm will come to thee.'

So they parted; and the young man pursued his way until, being about to turn the corner by the meeting-house, he looked back, and saw the head of Faith still peeping after him, with a melancholy air, in spite of her pink ribbons.

'Poor little Faith!' thought he, for his heart smote him.

'What a wretch am I to leave her on such an errand! She talks of dreams, too. Methought, as she spoke, there was trouble in her face, as if a dream had warned her what work is to be done tonight. But, no, no! 'twould kill her to think it. Well, she's a blessed angel on Earth, and after this one night, I'll cling to her skirts and follow her to heaven.'

With this excellent resolve for the future, Goodman Brown felt himself justified in making more haste on his present evil purpose. He had taken a dreary road, darkened by all the gloomiest trees of the forest which barely stood aside to let the narrow path creep through, and closed immediately behind. It was all as lonely as could be; and there is this peculiarity in such a solitude that the traveller knows not who may be concealed by the innumerable trunks and the thick boughs overhead, so that, with lonely footsteps, he may yet be passing through an unseen multitude.

'There may be a devilish Indian behind every tree,' said Goodman Brown to himself; and he glanced fearfully behind him as he added, 'What if the devil himself should be at my very elbow!'

His head being turned back, he passed a crook of the road, and looking forward again, beheld the figure of a man, in grave and decent attire, seated at the foot of an old tree. He arose at Goodman Brown's approach, and walked onward, side by side with him.

'You are late, Goodman Brown,' said he. 'The clock of the Old South was striking as I came through Boston, and that is full fifteen minutes agone.'

'Faith kept me back awhile,' replied the young man,

with a tremor in his voice, caused by the sudden appearance of his companion, though not wholly unexpected.

It was now deep dusk in the forest, and deepest in that part of it where these two were journeying. As nearly as could be discerned, the second traveller was about fifty years old, apparently in the same rank of life as Goodman Brown, and bearing a considerable resemblance to him, though perhaps more in expression than features. Still, they might have been taken for father and son. And yet, though the elder person was as simply clad as the younger, and as simple in manner too, he had an indescribable air of one who knew the world, and would not have felt abashed at the governor's dinner-table, or in King William's Court, were it possible that his affairs should call him thither. But the only thing about him that could be fixed upon as remarkable was his staff, which bore the likeness of a great black snake so curiously wrought that it might almost be seen to twist and wriggle itself, like a living serpent. This, of course, must have been an ocular deception, assisted by the uncertain light.

'Come, Goodman Brown!' cried his fellow-traveller, 'this is a dull pace for the beginning of a journey. Take my staff, if you are so soon weary.'

'Friend,' said the other, exchanging his slow pace for a full stop, 'having kept covenant by meeting thee here, it is my purpose now to return whence I came. I have scruples, touching the matter thou wot'st of.'

'Sayest thou so?' replied he of the serpent, smiling apart. 'Let us walk on, nevertheless, reasoning as we go, and if I convince thee not, thou shalt turn back. We are but a little way in the forest, yet.'

'Too far, too far!' exclaimed the goodman, unconsciously resuming his walk. 'My father never went into the woods on such an errand, nor his father before him. We have been a race of honest men and good Christians since the days of the martyrs. And shall I be the first of the name of Brown that ever took this path, and kept –'

'Such company, thou wouldst say,' observed the elder person, interpreting his pause. 'Well said, Goodman Brown! I have been as well acquainted with your family as with ever a one among the Puritans, and that's no trifle to say. I helped your grandfather, the constable, when he lashed the Quaker woman so smartly through the streets of Salem. And it was I that brought your father a pitch-pine knot, kindled at my own hearth, to set fire to an Indian village, in King Philip's war. They were my good friends both, and many a pleasant walk have we had along this path, and returned merrily after midnight. I would fain be friends with you, for their sake.'

'If it be as thou sayest,' replied Goodman Brown, 'I marvel they never spoke of these matters. Or, verily, I marvel not, seeing that the least rumour of the sort would have driven them from New England. We are a people of prayer, and good works to boot, and abide no such wickedness.'

'Wickedness or not,' said the traveller with the twisted staff, 'I have a very general acquaintance here in New England. The deacons of many a church have drunk the communion wine with me, the selectmen of divers towns make me their chairman, and a majority of the Great and General Court are firm supporters of my interest. The governor and I, too – but these are state secrets.'

'Can this be so!' cried Goodman Brown, with a stare of amazement at his undisturbed companion. 'Howbeit, I have nothing to do with the governor and council – they have their own ways, and are no rule for a simple husbandman like me. But, were I to go on with thee, how should I meet the eye of that good old man, our minister, at Salem village? Oh, his voice would make me tremble, both Sabbath day and lecture day!'

Thus far, the elder traveller had listened with due gravity, but now burst into a fit of irrepressible mirth, shaking himself so violently that his snake-like staff actually seemed to wriggle in sympathy.

'Ha! ha! ha!' shouted he, again and again; then composing himself, 'Well, go on, Goodman Brown, go on; but pr'y thee, don't kill me with laughing!'

'Well, then, to end the matter at once,' said Goodman Brown, considerably nettled, 'there is my wife, Faith. It would break her dear little heart, and I'd rather break my own!'

'Nay, if that be the case,' answered the other, 'e'en go thy ways, Goodman Brown. I would not, for twenty old women like the one hobbling before us, that Faith should come to any harm.'

As he spoke, he pointed his staff at a female figure on the path, in whom Goodman Brown recognised a very pious and exemplary dame who had taught him his catechism in youth, and was still his moral and spiritual adviser, jointly with the minister and Deacon Gookin.

'A marvel, truly, that Goody Cloyse should be so far in the wilderness at nightfall!' said he. 'But, with your leave, friend, I shall take a cut through the woods, until we have left this Christian woman behind. Being a stranger to you, she might ask whom I was consorting with, and whither I was going.'

'Be it so,' said his fellow-traveller. 'Betake you to the woods, and let me keep the path.'

Accordingly, the young man turned aside, but took care to watch his companion who advanced softly along the road until he had come within a staff's length of the old dame. She, meanwhile, was making the best of her way, with singular speed for so aged a woman, and mumbling some indistinct words – a prayer, doubtless – as she went. The traveller put forth his staff, and touched her withered neck with what seemed the serpent's tail.

'The devil!' screamed the pious old lady.

'Then Goody Cloyse knows her old friend?' observed the traveller, confronting her, and leaning on his writhing stick.

'Ah, forsooth, and is it your worship, indeed?' cried the good dame. 'Yea, truly is it, and in the very image of my old gossip, Goodman Brown, the grandfather of the silly fellow that now is. But – would your worship believe it? – my broomstick hath strangely disappeared, stolen, as I suspect, by that unhanged witch, Goody Cory, and that, too, when I was all anointed with the juice of smallage and cinquefoil and wolfsbane –'

'Mingled with fine wheat and the fat of a newborn babe,' said the shape of old Goodman Brown.

'Ah, your worship knows the recipe,' cried the old lady, cackling aloud. 'So, as I was saying, being all ready for the meeting, and no horse to ride on, I made up my mind to foot it, for they tell me there is a nice young man to be taken into communion tonight. But now your good worship will lend me your arm, and we shall be there in a twinkling.'

'That can hardly be,' answered her friend. 'I may not spare you my arm, Goody Cloyse, but here is my staff, if you will.'

So saying, he threw it down at her feet, where, perhaps, it assumed life, being one of the rods which its owner had formerly lent to the Egyptian magi. Of this fact, however, Goodman Brown could not take cognisance. He had cast up his eyes in astonishment, and looking down again, beheld neither Goody Cloyse nor the serpentine staff, but his fellow-traveller alone, who waited for him as calmly as if nothing had happened.

'That old woman taught me my catechism!' said the young man, and there was a world of meaning in this simple comment.

They continued to walk onward, while the elder traveller exhorted his companion to make good speed and persevere in the path, discoursing so aptly that his arguments seemed rather to spring up in the bosom of his auditor than to be suggested by himself. As they went, he plucked a branch of maple to serve for a walking-stick, and began to strip it of the twigs and little boughs which were wet with evening dew. The moment his fingers touched them, they became strangely withered and dried up, as with a week's sunshine. Thus the pair proceeded, at a good free pace, until suddenly, in a gloomy hollow of the road, Goodman Brown sat himself down on the stump of a tree, and refused to go any further.

'Friend,' said he, stubbornly, 'my mind is made up.

Not another step will I budge on this errand. What if a wretched old woman do choose to go to the devil, when I thought she was going to heaven! Is that any reason why I should quit my dear Faith, and go after her?'

'You will think better of this, by and by,' said his acquaintance, composedly. 'Sit here and rest yourself awhile, and when you feel like moving again, there is my staff to help you along.'

Without more words, he threw his companion the maple stick, and was as speedily out of sight as if he had vanished into the deepening gloom. The young man sat a few moments by the roadside, applauding himself greatly, and thinking with how clear a conscience he should meet the minister in his morning walk, nor shrink from the eye of good old Deacon Gookin. And what calm sleep would be his that very night, which was to have been spent so wickedly, but purely and sweetly now, in the arms of Faith! Amidst these pleasant and praiseworthy meditations, Goodman Brown heard the tramp of horses along the road, and deemed it advisable to conceal himself within the verge of the forest, conscious of the guilty purpose that had brought him thither, though now so happily turned from it.

On came the hoof tramps and the voices of the riders, two grave old voices, conversing soberly as they drew near. These mingled sounds appeared to pass along the road, within a few yards of the young man's hiding place; but owing, doubtless, to the depth of the gloom, at that particular spot, neither the travellers nor their steeds were visible. Though their figures brushed the small boughs by the wayside, it could not be seen that they intercepted, even for a moment, the faint gleam from the strip of bright sky, athwart which they must have passed. Goodman Brown alternately crouched and stood on tiptoe, pulling aside the branches, and thrusting forth his head as far as he durst, without discerning so much as a shadow. It vexed him the more, because he could have sworn, were such a thing possible, that he recognised the voices of the minister and Deacon Gookin, jogging along quietly, as they were wont to do when bound to some ordination or ecclesiastical council. While yet within hearing, one of the riders stopped to pluck a switch.

'Of the two, reverend sir,' said the voice like the deacon's, 'I had rather miss an ordination dinner than tonight's meeting. They tell me that some of our community are to be here from Falmouth and beyond, and others from Connecticut and Rhode Island, besides several of the Indian powwows who, after their fashion, know almost as much devilry as the best of us. Moreover, there is a goodly young woman to be taken into communion.'

'Mighty well, Deacon Gookin!' replied the solemn old tones of the minister. 'Spur up, or we shall be late. Nothing can be done, you know, until I get on the ground.'

The hoofs clattered again, and the voices, talking so strangely in the empty air, passed on through the forest, where no church had ever been gathered, nor solitary Christian prayed. Whither, then, could these holy men be journeying, so deep into the heathen wilderness? Young Goodman Brown caught hold of a tree for support, being ready to sink down on the ground, faint and overburdened with the heavy sickness of his heart. He looked up to the sky, doubting whether there really was a heaven above him. Yet, there was the blue arch, and the stars brightening in it.

'With heaven above, and Faith below, I will yet stand firm against the devil!' cried Goodman Brown.

While he still gazed upwards, into the deep arch of the firmament, and had lifted his hands to pray, a cloud, though no wind was stirring, hurried across the zenith, and hid the brightening stars. The blue sky was still visible, except directly overhead where this black mass of cloud was sweeping swiftly northward. Aloft in the air, as if from the depths of the cloud, came a confused and doubtful sound of voices. Once, the listener fancied that he could distinguish the accents of townspeople of his own, men and women, both pious and ungodly, many of whom he had met at the Communion table, and had seen others rioting at the tavern. The next moment, so indistinct were the sounds, he doubted whether he had heard aught but the murmur of the old forest, whispering without a wind. Then came a stronger swell of those familiar tones, heard daily in the sunshine at Salem village, but never, until now, from a cloud of night. There was one voice, of a young woman, uttering lamentations, yet with an uncertain sorrow, and entreating for some favour, which, perhaps, it would grieve her to obtain. And all the unseen multitude, both saints and sinners, seemed to encourage her onward.

'Faith!' shouted Goodman Brown, in a voice of agony and desperation; and the echoes of the forest mocked him, crying – 'Faith! Faith!' as if bewildered wretches were seeking her, all through the wilderness.

The cry of grief, rage, and terror, was yet piercing the night when the unhappy husband held his breath for a response. There was a scream, drowned immediately in a louder murmur of voices, fading into far-off laughter as the dark cloud swept away, leaving the clear and silent sky above Goodman Brown. But something fluttered lightly down through the air, and caught on the branch of a tree. The young man seized it, and beheld a pink ribbon.

'My Faith is gone!' cried he, after one stupefied moment. 'There is no good on Earth, and sin is but a name. Come, devil! for to thee is this world given.'

And maddened with despair, so that he laughed loud and long, did Goodman Brown grasp his staff and set forth again, at such a rate that he seemed to fly along the forest path rather than to walk or run. The road grew wilder and drearier, and more faintly traced, and vanished at length, leaving him in the heart of the dark wilderness, still rushing onward, with the instinct that guides mortal man to evil. The whole forest was peopled with frightful sounds: the creaking of the trees, the howling of wild beasts, and the yell of Indians, while, sometimes, the wind tolled like a distant church-bell, and sometimes gave a broad roar around the traveller as if all Nature were laughing him to scorn. But he was himself the chief horror of the scene, and shrank not from its other horrors.

'Ha! ha! ha!' roared Goodman Brown, when the wind laughed at him. 'Let us hear which will laugh loudest! Think not to frighten me with your devilry! Come witch, come wizard, come Indian powwow, come devil himself! and here comes Goodman Brown. You may as well fear him as he fear you!'

In truth, all through the haunted forest, there could be nothing more frightful than the figure of Goodman Brown. On he flew, among the black pines, brandishing his staff with frenzied gestures, now giving vent to an inspiration of horrid blasphemy, and now shouting forth such laughter as set all the echoes of the forest laughing like demons around him. The fiend in his own shape is less hideous than when he rages in the breast of man. Thus sped the demoniac on his course until, quivering among the trees, he saw a red light before him, as when the felled trunks and branches of a clearing have been set on fire and throw up their lurid blaze against the sky at the hour of midnight. He paused, in a lull of the tempest that had driven him onward, and heard the swell of what seemed a hymn, rolling solemnly from a distance, with the weight of many voices. He knew the tune; it was a familiar one in the choir of the village meeting-house. The verse died heavily away, and was lengthened by a chorus, not of human voices, but of all the sounds of the benighted wilderness, pealing in awful harmony together. Goodman Brown cried out, and his cry was lost to his own ear by its unison with the cry of the desert.

In the interval of silence, he stole forward until the light glared full upon his eyes. At one extremity of an open space, hemmed in by the dark wall of the forest, arose a rock, bearing some rude, natural resemblance either to an altar or a pulpit, and surrounded by four blazing pines, their tops aflame, their stems untouched, like candles at an evening meeting. The mass of foliage that had overgrown the summit of the rock was all on fire, blazing high into the night, and fitfully illuminating the whole field. Each pendent twig and leafy festoon was in a blaze. As the red light arose and fell, a numerous congregation alternately shone forth, then disappeared in shadow, and again grew, as it were, out of the darkness, peopling the heart of the solitary woods at once.

'A grave and dark-clad company!' quoth Goodman Brown.

In truth, they were such. Among them, quivering to and fro, between gloom and splendour, appeared faces that would be seen next day at the council-board of the province, and others which, Sabbath after Sabbath, looked devoutly heavenward and benignantly over the crowded pews from the holiest pulpits in the land. Some affirm that the lady of the governor was there. At least, there were high dames well known to her, and wives of honoured husbands, and widows, a great multitude, and ancient maidens, all of excellent repute, and fair young girls who trembled lest their mothers should espy them. Either the sudden gleams of light flashing over the obscure field bedazzled Goodman Brown, or he recognised a score of the church members of Salem village, famous for their special sanctity. Good old Deacon Gookin had arrived, and waited at the skirts of that venerable saint, his revered pastor. But, irreverently consorting with these grave, reputable, and pious people, these elders of the church, these chaste dames and dewy virgins, there were men of dissolute lives and women of spotted fame, wretches given over to all mean and filthy vice, and suspected even of horrid crimes. It was strange to see that the good shrank not from the wicked, nor were the sinners abashed by the saints. Scattered, also, among their pale-faced enemies, were the Indian priests, or powwows, who had often scared their native forest with more hideous incantations than any known to English witchcraft.

'But, where is Faith?' thought Goodman Brown, and, as hope came into his heart, he trembled.

Another verse of the hymn arose, a slow and mournful strain, such as the pious love, but joined to words which expressed all that our nature can conceive of sin, and darkly hinted at far more. Unfathomable to mere mortals is the lore of fiends. Verse after verse was sung, and still the chorus of the desert swelled between, like the deepest tone of a mighty organ. And, with the final peal of that dreadful anthem, there came a sound, as if the roaring wind, the rushing streams, the howling beasts, and every other voice of the unconverted wilderness, were mingling and according with the voice of guilty man, in homage to the prince of all. The four blazing pines threw up a loftier flame, and obscurely discovered shapes and visages of horror on the smoke wreaths, above the impious assembly. At the same moment, the fire on the rock shot redly forth, and formed a glowing arch above its base where now appeared a figure. With reverence be it spoken, the figure bore no slight similitude, both in garb and manner, to some grave divine of the New England churches.

'Bring forth the converts!' cried a voice that echoed through the field and rolled into the forest.

At the word, Goodman Brown stepped forth from the shadow of the trees, and approached the congregation, with whom he felt a loathful brotherhood by the sympathy of all that was wicked in his heart. He could have well-nigh sworn that the shape of his own dead father beckoned him to advance, looking downwards from a smoke wreath, while a woman, with dim features of despair, threw out her hand to warn him back. Was it his mother? But he had no power to retreat one step, nor to resist, even in thought, when the minister and good old Deacon Gookin seized his arms, and led him to the blazing rock. Thither came also the slender form of a veiled female, led between Goody Cloyse, that pious teacher of the catechism, and Martha Carrier, who had received the devil's promise to be queen of hell. A rampant hag was she! And there stood the proselytes, beneath the canopy of fire.

'Welcome, my children,' said the dark figure, 'to the communion of your race! Ye have found, thus young, your nature and your destiny. My children, look behind you!'

They turned; and flashing forth, as it were, in a sheet of flame, the fiend-worshippers were seen, the smile of welcome gleamed darkly on every visage.

'There,' resumed the sable form, 'are all whom ye have reverenced from youth. Ye deemed them holier than yourselves, and shrank from your own sin, contrasting it with their lives of righteousness and prayerful aspirations heavenward. Yet, here are they all, in my worshipping assembly! This night it shall be granted you to know their secret deeds: how hoary-bearded elders of the church have whispered wanton words to the young maids of their households; how many a woman, eager for widow's weeds, has given her husband a drink at bedtime, and let him sleep his last sleep in her bosom; how beardless youths have made haste to inherit their fathers' wealth;

and how fair damsels – blush not, sweet ones! – have dug little graves in the garden, and bidden me, the sole guest, to an infant's funeral. By the sympathy of your human hearts for sin, ye shall scent out all the places – whether in church, bedchamber, street, field, or forest – where crime has been committed, and shall exult to behold the whole Earth one stain of guilt, one mighty blood spot. Far more than this! It shall be yours to penetrate, in every bosom, the deep mystery of sin, the fountain of all wicked arts, and which inexhaustibly supplies more evil impulses than human power – than my power, at its utmost! – can make manifest in deeds. And now, my children, look upon each other.'

They did so, and, by the blaze of the hell-kindled torches, the wretched man beheld his Faith, and the wife her husband, trembling before that unhallowed altar.

'Lo! there ye stand, my children,' said the figure, in a deep and solemn tone, almost sad with its despairing awfulness, as if his once angelic nature could yet mourn for our miserable race. 'Depending upon one another's hearts, ye had still hoped that virtue were not all a dream. Now are ye undeceived! Evil is the nature of mankind. Evil must be your only happiness. Welcome, again, my children, to the communion of your race!'

'Welcome!' repeated the fiend-worshippers, in one cry of despair and triumph.

And there they stood, the only pair, as it seemed, who were yet hesitating on the verge of wickedness in this dark world. A basin was hollowed, naturally, in the rock. Did it contain water, reddened by the lurid light? or was it blood? or, perchance, a liquid flame? Herein did the shape of evil dip his hand, and prepare to lay the mark of baptism upon their foreheads that they might be partakers of the mystery of sin, more conscious of the secret guilt of others, both in deed and thought, than they could now be of their own. The husband cast one look at his pale wife, and Faith at him. What polluted wretches would the next glance show them to each other, shuddering alike at what they disclosed and what they saw!

'Faith! Faith!' cried the husband. 'Look up to heaven, and resist the wicked one!'

Whether Faith obeyed, he knew not. Hardly had he spoken when he found himself amid calm night and solitude, listening to a roar of the wind which died heavily away through the forest. He staggered against the rock, and felt it chill and damp, while a hanging twig, that had been all on fire, besprinkled his cheek with the coldest dew.

The next morning, young Goodman Brown came slowly into the street of Salem village, staring around him like a bewildered man. The good old minister was taking a walk along the graveyard to get an appetite for breakfast and meditate his sermon, and bestowed a blessing, as he passed, on Goodman Brown. He shrank from the venerable saint, as if to avoid an anathema. Old Deacon Gookin was at domestic worship, and the holy words of his prayer were heard through the open window. 'What God doth the wizard pray to?' quoth Goodman Brown. Goody Cloyse, that excellent old Christian, stood in the early sunshine at her own lattice, catechising a little girl who had brought her a pint of morning's milk. Goodman Brown snatched away the child, as from the grasp of the fiend himself. Turning the corner by the meeting-house, he spied the head of Faith, with the pink ribbons, gazing anxiously forth, and bursting into such joy at sight of him that she skipped along the street and almost kissed her husband before the whole village. But Goodman Brown looked sternly and sadly into her face, and passed on without a greeting.

Had Goodman Brown fallen asleep in the forest, and only dreamt a wild dream of a witch-meeting?

Be it so, if you will. But, alas! it was a dream of evil omen for young Goodman Brown. A stern, a sad, a darkly meditative, a distrustful, if not a desperate man, did he become from the night of that fearful dream. On the Sabbath day, when the congregation were singing a holy psalm, he could not listen, because an anthem of sin rushed loudly upon his ear, and drowned all the blessed strain. When the minister spoke from the pulpit, with power and fervid eloquence and, with his hand on the open Bible, of the sacred truths of our religion, and of saint-like lives and triumphant deaths, and of future bliss or misery unutterable, then did Goodman Brown turn pale, dreading, lest the roof should thunder down upon the grey blasphemer and his hearers. Often, awakening suddenly at midnight, he shrank from the bosom of Faith, and at morning or eventide, when the family knelt down at prayer, he scowled, and muttered to himself, and gazed sternly at his wife, and turned away. And when he had lived long and was borne to his grave a hoary corpse, followed by Faith, an aged woman, and children and grandchildren, a goodly procession, besides neighbours, not a few, they carved no hopeful verse upon his tombstone, for his dying hour was gloom.

A Select Party

A Man of Fancy made an entertainment at one of his castles in the air, and invited a select number of distinguished personages to favour him with their presence. The mansion, though less splendid than many that have been situated in the same region, was nevertheless of a magnificence such as is seldom witnessed by those acquainted only with terrestrial architecture. Its strong foundations and massive walls were quarried out of a ledge of heavy and sombre clouds which had hung brooding over the Earth, apparently as dense and ponderous as its own granite, throughout a whole autumnal day. Perceiving that the general effect was gloomy – so that the airy castle looked like a feudal fortress, or a monastery of the middle ages, or a State-prison of our own times, rather than the home of pleasure and repose which he intended it to be – the owner, regardless of expense, resolved to gild the exterior from top to bottom. Fortunately, there was just then a flood of evening sunshine in the air. This being gathered up and poured abundantly upon the roof and walls, imbued them with a kind of solemn cheerfulness, while the cupolas and pinnacles were made to glitter with the purest gold, and all the hundred windows gleamed with a glad light, as if the edifice itself were rejoicing in its heart. And now, if the people of the lower world chanced to be looking upwards, out of the turmoil of their petty perplexities, they probably mistook the castle in the air for a heap of sunset clouds to which the magic of light and shade had imparted the aspect of a fantastically constructed mansion. To such beholders it was unreal, because they lacked the imaginative faith. Had they been worthy to pass within its portal, they would have recognised the truth that the dominions which the spirit conquers for itself among unrealities become a thousand times more real than the earth whereon they stamp their feet, saying, 'This is solid and substantial! – this may be called a fact!'

At the appointed hour, the host stood in his great saloon to receive the company. It was a vast and noble room, the vaulted ceiling of which was supported by double rows of gigantic pillars that had been hewn entire out of masses of variegated clouds. So brilliantly were they polished, and so exquisitely wrought by the sculptor's skill, as to resemble the finest specimens of emerald, porphyry, opal, and chrysolite, thus producing a delicate richness of effect which their immense size rendered not incompatible with grandeur. To each of these pillars a meteor was suspended. Thousands of these ethereal lustres are continually wandering about the firmament, burning out to waste, yet capable of imparting a useful radiance to any person who has the art of converting them to domestic purposes. As managed in the saloon, they are far more economical than ordinary lamplight. Such, however, was the intensity of their blaze that it had been found expedient to cover each meteor with a globe of evening mist, thereby muffling the too-potent glow, and soothing it into a mild and comfortable splendour. It was like the brilliancy of a powerful, yet chastened, imagination: a light which seemed to hide whatever was unworthy to be noticed, and give effect to every beautiful and noble attribute. The guests, therefore, as they advanced up the centre of the saloon, appeared to better advantage than ever before in their lives.

The first that entered, with old-fashioned punctuality, was a venerable figure in the costume of bygone days, with his white hair flowing down over his shoulders, and a reverend beard upon his breast. He leant upon a staff, the tremulous stroke of which, as he set it carefully upon the floor, re-echoed through the saloon at every footstep. Recognising at once this celebrated personage, whom it had cost him a vast deal of trouble and research to discover, the host advanced nearly three quarters of the distance down between the pillars to meet and welcome him.

'Venerable sir,' said the Man of Fancy, bending to the floor, 'the honour of this visit would never be forgotten were my term of existence to be as happily prolonged as your own.'

The old gentleman received the compliment with gracious condescension; he then thrust up his spectacles over his forehead, and appeared to take a critical survey of the saloon.

'Never, within my recollection,' observed he, 'have I entered a more spacious and noble hall. But are you sure that it is built of solid materials, and that the structure will be permanent?'

'Oh, never fear, my venerable friend,' replied the host. 'In reference to a lifetime like your own, it is true, my castle may well be called a temporary edifice. But it will endure long enough to answer all the purposes for which it was erected.'

But we forget that the reader has not yet been made acquainted with the guest. It was no other than that universally accredited character so constantly referred to in all seasons of intense cold or heat – he that remembers the hot Sunday and the cold Friday – the witness of a past age, whose negative reminiscences find their way into every newspaper, yet whose antiquated and dusky abode is so overshadowed by accumulated years and crowded back by modern edifices that none but the Man of Fancy could have discovered it – it was, in short, that twin brother of Time, and great-grandfather of mankind, and hand-and-glove associate of all forgotten men and things, the Oldest Inhabitant. The host would willingly have drawn him into conversation, but succeeded only in eliciting a few remarks as to the oppressive atmosphere of this present summer evening, compared with one which the guest had experienced about four-score years ago. The old gentleman, in fact, was a good deal overcome by his journey among the clouds which, to a frame so earth-encrusted by long continuance in a lower region, was unavoidably more fatiguing than to younger spirits. He was therefore conducted to an easy chair, well cushioned, and stuffed with vaporous softness, and left to take a little repose.

The Man of Fancy now discerned another guest, who stood so quietly in the shadow of one of the pillars that he might easily have been overlooked.

'My dear sir,' exclaimed the host, grasping him warmly by the hand, 'allow me to greet you as the hero of the evening. Pray do not take it as an empty compliment, for if there were not another guest in my castle, it would be entirely pervaded with your presence!'

'I thank you,' answered the unpretending stranger, 'but, though you happened to overlook me, I have not just arrived. I came very early, and, with your permission, shall remain after the rest of the company have retired.'

And who does the reader imagine was this unobtrusive guest? It was the famous performer of acknowledged impossibilities – a character of superhuman capacity and virtue, and, if his enemies are to be credited, of no less remarkable weaknesses and defects. With a generosity of which he alone sets us the example, we will glance merely at his nobler attributes. He it is, then, who prefers the interests of others to his own, and a humble station to an exalted one. Careless of fashion, custom, the opinions of men, and the influence of the press, he assimilates his life to the standard of ideal rectitude, and thus proves himself the one independent citizen of our free country. In point of ability, many people declare him to be the only mathematician capable of squaring the circle; the only mechanic acquainted with the principle of perpetual motion; the only scientific philosopher who can compel water to run uphill; the only writer of the age whose genius is equal to the production of an epic poem; and, finally – so various are his accomplishments – the only professor of gymnastics who has succeeded in jumping down his own throat. With all these talents, however, he is so far from being considered a member of good society that it is the severest censure of any fashionable assemblage to affirm that this remarkable individual was present. Public orators, lecturers, and theatrical performers, particularly eschew his company. For special reasons we are not at liberty to disclose his name, and shall mention only one other trait – a most singular phenomenon in natural philosophy – that when he happens to cast his eyes upon a looking-glass, he beholds Nobody reflected there!

Several other guests now made their appearance, and

among them, chattering with immense volubility, a brisk little gentleman of universal vogue in private society, and not unknown in the public journals, under the title of Monsieur On-Dit. The name would seem to indicate a Frenchman; but, whatever be his country, he is thoroughly versed in all the languages of the day, and can express himself quite as much to the purpose in English as in any other tongue. No sooner were the ceremonies of salutation over than this talkative little person put his mouth to the host's ear, and whispered three secrets of state, an important piece of commercial intelligence, and a rich item of fashionable scandal. He then assured the Man of Fancy that he would not fail to circulate in the society of the lower world a minute description of this magnificent castle in the air, and of the festivities at which he had the honour to be a guest. So saying, Monsieur On-Dit made his bow and hurried from one to another of the company, with all of whom he seemed to be acquainted, and to possess some topic of interest or amusement for every individual. Coming at last to the Oldest Inhabitant, who was slumbering comfortably in the easy chair, he applied his mouth to that venerable ear.

'What do you say?' cried the old gentleman, starting from his nap, and putting up his hand to serve the purpose of an ear-trumpet.

Monsieur On-Dit bent forward again, and repeated his communication.

'Never, within my memory,' exclaimed the Oldest Inhabitant, lifting his hands in astonishment, 'has so remarkable an incident been heard of!'

Now came in the Clerk of the Weather who had been

invited out of deference to his official station, although the host was well aware that his conversation was likely to contribute but little to the general enjoyment. He soon, indeed, got into a corner with his acquaintance of long ago, the Oldest Inhabitant, and began to compare notes with him in reference to the great storms, gales of wind, and other atmospherical facts that had occurred during a century past. It rejoiced the Man of Fancy that his venerable and much-respected guest had met with so congenial an associate. Entreating them both to make themselves perfectly at home, he now turned to receive the Wandering Jew. This personage, however, had latterly grown so common, by mingling in all sorts of society, and appearing at the beck of every entertainer, that he could hardly be deemed a proper guest in a very exclusive circle. Besides, being covered with dust from his continual wanderings along the highways of the world, he really looked out of place in a dress party, so that the host felt relieved of an incommodity when the restless individual in question, after a brief stay, took his departure on a ramble towards Oregon.

The portal was now thronged by a crowd of shadowy people with whom the Man of Fancy had been acquainted in his visionary youth. He had invited them hither for the sake of observing how they would compare, whether advantageously or otherwise, with the real characters to whom his maturer life had introduced him. They were beings of crude imagination, such as glide before a young man's eye and pretend to be actual inhabitants of the Earth: the wise and witty, with whom he would hereafter hold intercourse; the generous and heroic friends whose devotion would be requited with his own; the beautiful dream-woman who would become the helpmate of his human toils and sorrows, and at once the source and partaker of his happiness. Alas! it is not good for the full-grown man to look too closely at these old acquaintances, but rather to reverence them at a distance, through the medium of years that have gathered duskily between. There was something laughably untrue in their pompous stride and exaggerated sentiment; they were neither human, nor tolerable likenesses of humanity, but fantastic masquers, rendering heroism and nature alike ridiculous by the grave absurdity of their pretensions to such attributes. And as for the peerless dream-lady, behold! there advanced up the saloon, with a movement like a jointed doll, a sort of wax figure of an angel – a creature as cold as moonshine – an artifice in petticoats, with an intellect of pretty phrases, and only the semblance of a heart – yet, in all these particulars, the true type of a young man's imaginary mistress. Hardly could the host's punctilious courtesy restrain a smile as he paid his respects to this unreality, and met the sentimental glance with which the Dream sought to remind him of their former love-passages.

'No, no, fair lady,' murmured he, betwixt sighing and smiling; 'my taste is changed! I have learnt to love what Nature makes, better than my own creations in the guise of womanhood.'

'Ah, false one!' shrieked the dream-lady, pretending to faint, but dissolving into thin air, out of which came the deplorable murmur of her voice, 'your inconstancy has annihilated me!'

'So be it,' said the cruel Man of Fancy to himself. 'And a good riddance, too!'

Together with these shadows, and from the same region, there came an uninvited multitude of shapes, which, at any time during his life, had tormented the Man of Fancy in his moods of morbid melancholy, or had haunted him in the delirium of fever. The walls of his castle in the air were not dense enough to keep them out, nor would the strongest of earthly architecture have availed to their exclusion. Here were those forms of dim terror which had beset him at the entrance of life, waging warfare with his hopes. Here were strange uglinesses of earlier date, such as haunt children in the night-time. He was particularly startled by the vision of a deformed old black woman whom he imagined as lurking in the garret of his native home, and who, when he was an infant, had once come to his bedside and grinned at him in the crisis of a scarlet fever. This same black shadow, with others almost as hideous, now glided among the pillars of the magnificent saloon, grinning recognition, until the man shuddered anew at the forgotten terrors of his childhood. It amused him, however, to observe the black woman, with the mischievous caprice peculiar to such beings, steal up to the chair of the Oldest Inhabitant, and peep into his half-dreamy mind.

'Never within my memory,' muttered that venerable personage, aghast, 'did I see such a face!'

Almost immediately after the unrealities just described, arrived a number of guests whom incredulous readers may be inclined to rank equally among creatures of imagination. The most noteworthy were an incorruptible

Patriot, a Scholar without pedantry, a Priest without worldly ambition, and a Beautiful Woman without pride or coquetry, a Married Pair whose life had never been disturbed by incongruity of feeling, a Reformer, untrammelled by his theory, and a Poet who felt no jealousy towards other votaries of the lyre. In truth, however, the host was not one of the cynics who consider these patterns of excellence, without the fatal flaw, such rarities in the world; and he had invited them to his select party chiefly out of humble deference to the judgement of society which pronounces them almost impossible to be met with.

'In my younger days,' observed the Oldest Inhabitant, 'such characters might be seen at the corner of every street.'

Be that as it might, these specimens of perfection proved to be not half so entertaining companions as people with the ordinary allowance of faults.

But now appeared a stranger whom the host had no sooner recognised than, with an abundance of courtesy unravished on any other, he hastened down the whole length of the saloon in order to pay him emphatic honour. Yet he was a young man in poor attire, with no insignia of rank or acknowledged eminence, nor anything to distinguish him among the crowd except a high, white forehead, beneath which a pair of deep-set eyes were glowing with warm light. It was such a light as never illuminates the Earth, save when a great heart burns as the household fire of a grand intellect. And who was he? – who but the Master Genius for whom our country is looking anxiously into the mist of Time, as destined to fulfil the great mission of creating an American literature, hewing it, as it were, out of the unwrought granite of our intellectual quarries. From him, whether moulded in the form of an epic poem, or assuming a guise altogether new, as the spirit itself may determine, we are to receive our first great original work which shall do all that remains to be achieved for our glory among the nations. How this child of a mighty destiny had been discovered by the Man of Fancy it is of little consequence to mention. Suffice it that he dwells as yet unhonoured among men, unrecognised by those who have known him from his cradle; the noble countenance, which should be distinguished by a halo diffused around it, passes daily amid the throng of people, toiling and troubling themselves about the trifles of a moment – and none pays reverence to the worker of immortality. Nor does it matter much to him, in his triumph over all the ages, though a generation or two of his own times shall do themselves the wrong to disregard him.

By this time, Monsieur On-Dit had caught up the stranger's name and destiny, and was busily whispering the intelligence among the other guests.

'Pshaw!' said one, 'there can never be an American Genius.'

'Pish!' cried another, 'we have already as good poets as any in the world. For my part, I desire to see no better.'

And the Oldest Inhabitant, when it was proposed to introduce him to the Master Genius, begged to be excused, observing that a man who had been honoured with the acquaintance of Dwight, and Freneau, and Joel Barlow[1], might be allowed a little austerity of taste.

The saloon was now fast filling up by the arrival of other remarkable characters, among whom were noticed Davy Jones[2], the distinguished nautical personage, and a rude, carelessly dressed, harum-scarum sort of elderly fellow, known by the nickname of Old Harry[3]. The latter, however, after being shown to a dressing-room, re-appeared with his grey hair nicely combed, his clothes brushed, a clean dicky on his neck, and altogether so changed in aspect as to merit the more respectful appellation of Venerable Henry. John Doe and Richard Roe[4] came arm in arm, accompanied by a Man of Straw, a fictitious endorser, and several persons who had no existence except as voters in closely contested elections. The celebrated Seatsfield[5], who now entered, was at first supposed to belong to the same brotherhood until he made it apparent that he was a real man of flesh and blood, and had his earthly domicile in Germany. Among the latest comers, as might reasonably be expected, arrived a guest from the far future.

'Do you know him? – do you know him?' whispered Monsieur On-Dit, who seemed to be acquainted with everybody. 'He is the representative of Posterity – the man of an age to come!'

'And how came he here?' asked a figure, who was evidently the prototype of the fashion plate in a magazine, and might be taken to represent the vanities of the passing moment. 'The fellow infringes upon our rights by coming before his time.'

'But you forget where we are,' answered the Man of Fancy, who overheard the remark. 'The lower earth, it is true, will be forbidden ground to him for many long years hence, but a castle in the air is a sort of no man's land where Posterity may make acquaintance with us on equal terms.'

No sooner was his identity known than a throng of guests gathered about Posterity, all expressing the most generous interest in his welfare, and many boasting of the sacrifices which they had made, or were willing to make, on his behalf. Some, with as much secrecy as possible, desired his judgement upon certain copies of verses, or great manuscript rolls of prose; others accosted him with the familiarity of old friends, taking it for granted that he was perfectly cognisant of their names and characters. At length, finding himself thus beset, Posterity was put quite beside his patience.

'Gentlemen, my good friends,' cried he, breaking loose from a misty poet who strove to hold him by the button, 'I pray you to attend to your own business, and leave me to take care of mine! I expect to owe you nothing, unless it be certain national debts, and other encumbrances and impediments, physical and moral, which I shall find it troublesome enough to remove from my path. As to your verses, pray read them to your contemporaries. Your names are as strange to me as your faces; and even were it otherwise – let me whisper you a secret – the cold, icy memory which one generation may retain of another, is but a poor recompense to barter life for. Yet, if your heart is set on being known to me, the surest, the only method is to live truly and wisely for your own age, whereby, if the native force be in you, you may likewise live for posterity!'

'It is nonsense,' murmured the Oldest Inhabitant who, as a man of the past, felt jealous that all notice should be withdrawn from himself to be lavished on the future, 'sheer nonsense, to waste so much thought on what only is to be!'

To divert the minds of his guests who were considerably abashed by this little incident, the Man of Fancy led them through several apartments of the castle, receiving their compliments upon the taste and varied magnificence that were displayed in each. One of these rooms was filled with moonlight, which did not enter through the window, but was the aggregate of all the moonshine that is scattered around the Earth on a summer night while no eyes are awake to enjoy its beauty. Airy spirits had gathered it up wherever they found it gleaming on the broad bosom of a lake, or silvering the meanders of a stream, or glimmering among the wind-stirred boughs of a wood, and had garnered it in this one spacious hall. Along the walls, illuminated by the mild intensity of the moonshine, stood a multitude of ideal statues, the original conceptions of the great works of ancient or modern art, which the sculptors did but imperfectly succeed in putting into marble. For it is not to be supposed that the pure idea of an immortal creation ceases to exist; it is only necessary to know where they are deposited, in order to obtain possession of them. In the alcoves of another vast apartment was arranged a splendid library, the volumes of which were inestimable because they consisted not of actual performances, but of the works which the authors only planned, without ever finding the happy season to achieve them. To take familiar instances, here were the untold tales of Chaucer's Canterbury Pilgrims, the unwritten cantos of *The Faerie*

Queene, the conclusion of Coleridge's *Christabel*, and the whole of Dryden's projected epic on the subject of King Arthur. The shelves were crowded, for it would not be too much to affirm that every author has imagined, and shaped out in his thought, more and far better works than those which actually proceeded from his pen. And here, likewise, were the unrealised conceptions of youthful poets who died of the very strength of their own genius, before the world had caught one inspired murmur from their lips.

When the peculiarities of the library and statue gallery were explained to the Oldest Inhabitant, he appeared infinitely perplexed, and exclaimed, with more energy than usual, that he had never heard of such a thing within his memory, and, moreover, did not at all understand how it could be.

'But my brain, I think,' said the good old gentleman, 'is getting not so clear as it used to be. You young folks, I suppose, can see your way through these strange matters. For my part, I give it up.'

'And so do I,' muttered the Old Harry. 'It is enough to puzzle the – Ahem!'

Making as little reply as possible to these observations, the Man of Fancy preceded the company to another noble saloon, the pillars of which were solid golden sunbeams, taken out of the sky in the first hour in the morning. Thus, as they retained all their living lustre, the room was filled with the most cheerful radiance imaginable, yet not too dazzling to be borne with comfort and delight. The windows were beautifully adorned with curtains, made of the many-coloured clouds of sunrise, all imbued with virgin light, and hanging in magnificent festoons from the ceiling to the floor. Moreover, there were fragments of rainbows scattered through the room, so that the guests, astonished at one another, reciprocally saw their heads made glorious by the seven primary hues; or, if they chose – as who would not? – they could grasp a rainbow in the air, and convert it to their own apparel and adornment. But the morning light and scattered rainbows were only a type and symbol of the real wonders of the apartment. By an influence akin to magic, yet perfectly natural, whatever means and opportunities of joy are neglected in the lower world had been carefully gathered up and deposited in the saloon of morning sunshine. As may well be conceived, therefore, there was material enough to supply not merely a joyous evening, but also a happy lifetime, to more than as many people as that spacious apartment could contain. The company seemed to renew their youth, while that pattern and proverbial standard of innocence, the Child Unborn, frolicked to and fro among them, communicating his own unwrinkled gaiety to all who had the good fortune to witness his gambols.

'My honoured friends,' said the Man of Fancy, after they had enjoyed themselves awhile, 'I am now to request your presence in the banqueting hall where a slight collation is awaiting you.'

'Ah, well said!' ejaculated a cadaverous figure who had been invited for no other reason than that he was pretty constantly in the habit of dining with Duke Humphrey[6]. 'I was beginning to wonder whether a castle in the air were provided with a kitchen.'

It was curious, in truth, to see how instantaneously the guests were diverted from the high moral enjoyments which they had been tasting with so much apparent zest, by a suggestion of the more solid as well as liquid delights of the festive board. They thronged eagerly in the rear of the host who now ushered them into a lofty and extensive hall, from end to end of which was arranged a table, glittering all over with innumerable dishes and drinking vessels of gold. It is an uncertain point, whether these rich articles of plate were made for the occasion, out of molten sunbeams, or recovered from the wrecks of Spanish galleons that had lain for ages at the bottom of the sea. The upper end of the table was overshadowed by a canopy, beneath which was placed a chair of elaborate magnificence, which the host himself declined to occupy, and besought his guests to assign it to the worthiest among them. As a suitable homage to his incalculable antiquity and eminent distinction, the post of honour was at first tendered to the Oldest Inhabitant. He, however, eschewed it, and requested the favour of a bowl of gruel at a side-table where he could refresh himself with a quiet nap. There was some little hesitation as to the next candidate, until Posterity took the Master Genius of our country by the hand, and led him to the chair of state, beneath the princely canopy. When once they beheld him in his true place, the company acknowledged the justice of the selection by a long thunder roll of vehement applause.

Then was served up a banquet, combining, if not all the delicacies of the season, yet all the rarities which careful purveyors had met with in the flesh, fish, and vegetable markets of the land of Nowhere. The bill of fare being unfortunately lost, we can only mention a phoenix, roasted in its own flames, cold potted birds of Paradise, ice-creams from the Milky Way, and whip-syllabubs and flummery from the Paradise of Fools, whereof there was a very great consumption. As for drinkables, the temperance-people contented themselves with water, as usual, but it was the water of the Fountain of Youth; the ladies sipped Nepenthe[7]; the lovelorn, the careworn, and the sorrow-stricken were supplied with brimming goblets of Lethe[8]; and it was shrewdly conjectured that a certain golden vase, from which only the more distinguished guests were invited to partake, contained nectar that had been mellowing ever since the days of classical mythology. The cloth being removed, the company, as usual, grew eloquent over their liquor, and delivered themselves of a succession of brilliant speeches – the task of reporting which we resign to the more adequate ability of Counsellor Gill, whose indispensable cooperation the Man of Fancy had taken the precaution to secure.

When the festivity of the banquet was at its most ethereal point, the Clerk of the Weather was observed to steal from the table, and thrust his head between the purple and golden curtains of one of the windows.

'My fellow-guests,' he remarked aloud, after carefully noting the signs of the night, 'I advise such of you as live at a distance to be going as soon as possible, for a thunderstorm is certainly at hand.'

'Mercy on me!' cried Mother Carey, who had left her brood of chickens, and come hither in gossamer drapery, with pink silk stockings. 'How shall I ever get home?'

All now was confusion and hasty departure, with but little superfluous leave-taking. The Oldest Inhabitant, however, true to the rule of those long-past days in which his courtesy had been studied, paused on the threshold of the meteor-lit hall to express his vast satisfaction at the entertainment.

'Never, within my memory,' observed the gracious old gentleman, 'has it been my good fortune to spend a pleasanter evening, or in more select society.'

The wind here took his breath away, whirled his three-cornered hat into infinite space, and drowned what further compliments it had been his purpose to bestow. Many of the company had bespoken will-o'-the-wisps to convoy them home, and the host, in his general beneficence, had engaged the Man in the Moon, with an immense horn lantern, to be the guide of such desolate spinsters as could do no better for themselves. But a blast of the rising tempest blew out all their lights in the twinkling of an eye. How, in the darkness that ensued, the guests contrived to get back to Earth, or whether the greater part of them contrived to get back at all, or are still wandering among clouds, mists, and puffs of tempestuous wind, bruised by the beams and rafters of the overthrown castle in the air, and deluded by all sorts of unrealities, are points that concern themselves much more than the writer or the public. People should think of these matters before they trust themselves on a pleasure-party into the realm of Nowhere.

NOTES

1. Theologian, scholar and writer Timothy Dwight (1752–1817) was the author of the poem *Greenfield Hill*; poet Philip Freneau (1752–1832) was a radical advocate of political democracy; Joel Barlow (1754–1812) was the author of *The Columbiad*, a lengthy and patriotic epic composed in heroic couplets. All three were key figures among the 'Hartford wits' of the late eighteenth century.

2. Davy Jones is a sailor's name for death or the devil. 'Davy Jones' locker' refers to the ocean, where the bodies of dead sailors are received.

3. Old Harry is a term for the devil.

4. John Doe is an expression for a hypothetical plaintiff, with Richard Roe being the corresponding defendant.

5. Writer Charles Sealsfield (1793–1864) was once mistakenly referred to as Seatsfield in an American newspaper and so was, as such, the 'celebrated Seatsfield'.

6. 'To dine with Duke Humphrey' is an expression meaning to have no dinner to go to, arising from the death of Humphrey, Duke of Gloucester and son of Henry IV, who, in life, was renowned for his great hospitality.

7. Nepenthe is a drug supposedly given to drive away care and to induce love.

8. In Greek mythology, Lethe is one of the rivers that flows through Hades; its waters, when drunk, were supposed to induce forgetfulness.

BIOGRAPHICAL NOTE

Nathaniel Hawthorne was born in Salem, Massachusetts in 1804, a descendant of Major William Hathorne, one of the Puritan settlers in America. William Hathorne is remembered for his persecution of the Quakers, and his son, John, as one of the magistrates during Salem's notorious witch-trials of 1692. Hawthorne (who adopted this spelling of the family name) spent a lonely childhood with his mother after the early death of his father, a sea-captain. He read widely as a child, and at school befriended Longfellow and the later president Franklin Pierce.

During his young adulthood, Hawthorne was a frequent contributor to periodicals, and had numerous short stories published, many of which appeared in the *Democratic Review*. His first novel, *Fanshawe*, was published anonymously in 1828 but received little critical attention. He followed this up with a number of works for children, and his short stories were collected in two volumes of *Twice-Told Tales* (1837; 1842).

In 1842 Hawthorne was introduced to members of the Transcendentalist Movement in Concord – notably Emerson, Thoreau and Alcott – but before long he grew dissatisfied with the Movement. His mixed response to Transcendentalism is conveyed in the novel *The Blithedale Romance* (1852). He married Sophia Peabody in 1842 and though they originally settled in Concord, large debts forced them to relocate to Salem with their now growing family. Unable to command the required income as a writer, Hawthorne entered employment as surveyor of the Port of Salem, a position he held from 1846 to 1849.

His most famous work, *The Scarlet Letter*, in which Hawthorne explored the notions of Puritan obsession and guilt, appeared in 1850. It is considered by many to be the first American psychological novel. It was followed in 1851 by *The House of the Seven Gables* – a remarkable tale of ancestral guilt. In 1853 Hawthorne's childhood friend Franklin Pierce became President and appointed Hawthorne American consul in Liverpool. Hawthorne thus lived in England for the ensuing four years, before moving to Italy where he wrote *The Marble Faun* (1860), his last completed novel. He then returned home to Concord, but died during a trip to the mountains with Franklin Pierce in 1864.

HESPERUS PRESS – 100 PAGES

Hesperus Press, as suggested by the Latin motto, is committed to bringing near what is far – far both in space and time. Works written by the greatest authors, and unjustly neglected or simply little known in the English-speaking world, are made accessible through new translations and a completely fresh editorial approach. Through these short classic works, each around 100 pages in length, the reader will be introduced to the greatest writers from all times and all cultures.

For more information on Hesperus Press, please visit our website: **www.hesperuspress.com**

ET REMOTISSIMA PROPE

SELECTED TITLES FROM HESPERUS PRESS

Gustave Flaubert *Memoirs of a Madman*

Alexander Pope *Scriblerus*

Ugo Foscolo *Last Letters of Jacopo Ortis*

Anton Chekhov *The Story of a Nobody*

Joseph von Eichendorff *Life of a Good-for-nothing*

Mark Twain *The Diary of Adam and Eve*

Giovanni Boccaccio *Life of Dante*

Victor Hugo *The Last Day of a Condemned Man*

Joseph Conrad *Heart of Darkness*

Edgar Allan Poe *Eureka*

Emile Zola *For a Night of Love*

Daniel Defoe *The King of Pirates*

Giacomo Leopardi *Thoughts*

Nikolai Gogol *The Squabble*

Franz Kafka *Metamorphosis*

Herman Melville *The Enchanted Isles*

Leonardo da Vinci *Prophecies*

Charles Baudelaire *On Wine and Hashish*

William Makepeace Thackeray *Rebecca and Rowena*

Wilkie Collins *Who Killed Zebedee?*

Théophile Gautier *The Jinx*

Charles Dickens *The Haunted House*

Luigi Pirandello *Loveless Love*

Fyodor Dostoevsky *Poor People*

E.T.A. Hoffmann *Mademoiselle de Scudéri*

Henry James *In the Cage*

Francis Petrarch *My Secret Book*

André Gide *Theseus*

D.H. Lawrence *The Fox*